BETWEEN BLADES AND BLOOD

CRIMSON ICE
BOOK 1

WILLOW FOX

SLOW BURN PUBLISHING

ONE

HARPER

Snow blanketed the city, making the roads dangerous, and yet, somehow, we still had classes to attend. It didn't matter that it was twenty below zero outside, with windchill, or that my fingers were freezing inside my gloves.

Buses on campus took us from the dorms to some of the buildings. But try to get on one of those buses in this frigid weather? Good luck.

Ditching class wasn't an option. I made that mistake during my first semester of freshman year. I wasn't going to do it again and risk my scholarship.

I needed a piping hot cup of coffee, but that was in the opposite direction of class. I trudged outside through the snow, my fur-lined boots keeping my feet warm. My legs, however, were quickly growing numb.

What was I doing walking to class in this blizzard? Would our teacher even show up?

"I hate winter," I grumble under my breath.

"What's that?" A male voice catches up with me as I wait to cross the street. The roads are slick; the plow hasn't come through this section yet. They're probably still trying to keep the highway from becoming treacherous.

I glance up at him. His dark eyes glint in the brightness of the snow surrounding us.

"It's cold," I say, stating the obvious. I'm practically hopping from one foot to the other, bouncing to keep warm. I swear I've seen him before on campus, but I don't recognize him from any of my classes.

Evergreen University campus isn't a small school, with more than twenty-thousand students in attendance, but you tend to recognize faces when you take the same route every day to class.

"It's winter," he says with a hearty laugh. It's deep and warm, and he offers me a friendly smile. The traffic light switches, and I hurry across the intersection, my feet slipping and sliding, and I nearly lose my footing.

The handsome stranger catches my arm, steadying me. "Careful," he warns, keeping me upright.

My heart pounds in my chest. "Thanks."

He has yet to release his grip as we cross the street.

"You can let go, I'm good," I say.

I feel the heat of his stare, and if my cheeks weren't red from the cold, I'd certainly be blushing.

"If you insist," he says, releasing his hold. The warmth that he possessed vanishes as quickly as it came, and I feel even chillier than before.

I can feel the heat of his stare as we walk, his gaze on me and then facing forward. Every so often, his arm brushes against mine through our thick jackets. It's an accident. I'm sure of it.

"Do you want to grab coffee?" he asks.

Perhaps it isn't an accident.

"I can't. I have to get to class."

Does he honestly think I'd be out in this cold if I didn't have to be? The windchill is brutal, making my cheeks sting. Even with the beanie on my head, covering my ears, I'm still frigid.

"I meant after. I'm Ashton," he introduces himself. "And you are?"

"Late for class," I say, glancing at him. His dark eyes warm me, but I don't have time for this, for him, for any of it. "It was nice meeting you, Ashton," I say as I approach the building.

"I didn't catch your name," Ashton says, his gaze hopeful as it lingers on me a little longer than necessary.

My gloved hand grabs the door handle. "That's because I didn't give it." I smirk. I yank open the door and am greeted with a gust of heat that slaps me in the face.

I hurry down the hallway, removing my hat and gloves, shoving them into my jacket pocket before unbuttoning the monstrosity. I head into the classroom and grab a seat in the middle of the auditorium.

"Hey, McKenna," Luca says, coming to sit beside me.

"Ricci," I say, calling him by his last name. He's nice-looking, and he knows it. Being a star hockey player for the university doesn't seem to hurt his dating life, either. He's got *player* written all over his smug face.

Why he wants to sit beside me is beyond comprehension. There are plenty of open seats in the auditorium. I retrieve my laptop from my backpack and power it up.

"Fun weekend?" he asks, and I swear he's only asking so that he can tell me all about his weekend.

"Yeah, it was great." I don't elaborate. My roommate, Quinn, and I don't exactly get along, and she likes to have boys over, which means I'm pretty much kicked out of the room when they're doing the no-pants dance.

Which seems to be every weekend and every chance that she gets to hook up with a guy.

The freshman requirement to live on campus in the dorms with a sophomore is the worst idea imaginable. Who thought it was a good idea? Some idiot who hadn't lived on campus in several decades.

"You should come to one of our parties," Luca says.

Is he actually inviting me to a party?

Why?

What's his motive, because I know he's not the least bit interested in me? In fact, if I didn't know any better, the reason he sits right beside me is to copy my notes during class. I'm pretty sure that's the only reason he sits next to me.

I'm a really good note-taker.

"I'll think about it," I say.

I smile politely and am relieved when our teacher enters the auditorium and class begins.

Luca seems like a decent guy, but his priorities are hockey, girls, and partying. I'm not sure if that's the exact order; he could put girls or partying first, but he's a decent hockey player, from what I've heard around campus. I've never been to one of their games, and I don't plan on showing up, either.

The minute class is over, I bundle back up into my hat, gloves, and oversized jacket. "Ready to brave the elements?" Luca asks. He's got on a black wool coat that doesn't look particularly warm.

"I should be asking you that," I say, glancing at him.

He gives me a wry grin, affixes a beanie to his head to keep warm, and slides his hands into his pockets. "I'm a snow owl," he says. "The cold doesn't bother me."

I snort under my breath. "Yeah, right," I mutter, unconvinced. He's right at my side, walking with me outside and across the quad to our next class. I don't have to cross any slushy streets at least, so there's little chance of slipping and falling, like earlier.

The walkway has been cleared, and there's salt that is finally melting some of the path. His breath is visible as he walks beside me, but he doesn't so much as shiver.

I'm hurrying outside, wanting to get out of the frigid weather. "Have a good day," he says as I head for the building.

"You too," I shout over my shoulder and grab the door handle.

He doesn't have class in the Fitzroy building but always walks with me to my next class. I've always assumed it's because he's in the Cooper building just past Fitzroy. I glance back through the glass windows and see him turning around, heading back in the direction where we just came from.

Did he forget something?

———

"Tell me if this is weird," I say to Kensley. We're both freshmen and have two classes together. We grab lunch at the on-campus deli and snag a table before it gets too crowded.

"Do tell," Kensley says, intrigued.

"Luca Ricci has been walking me to class for the past two weeks."

"What?" Kensley's eyes widen. "The center forward for Evergreen University. That's a little weird."

I shoot her a look. "That's not the weird part."

She smirks. "Continue."

"I thought he had class in the Cooper Building since he's been walking me to Fitzroy, but this morning, I saw him turn back around and head in the opposite direction."

"You could just ask him where his next class is," Kensley says, stating the obvious.

"Or?" I'm hoping she has another suggestion, something a little less direct. I don't want Luca Ricci to think I'm catching feelings for him, because I'm not.

"Follow him after he drops you off at class," Kensley suggests.

"I'm not stalking him."

"Right. Or we could go with option number three."

"Which is?"

"Hey, McKenna." Luca comes up from behind.

Kensley obviously saw him coming.

She should have warned me.

"Ricci," I say, staring at him. My mouth goes dry, all rational thought leaves my brain.

"I'm Kensley," my friend says, introducing herself.

"Luca," he says, giving a crooked smile and nod. "I was just about to grab lunch. Mind if I join you?"

"Not at all," Kensley says, answering before I have the opportunity to turn him down.

He heads for the counter, grabbing his food while I seethe at Kensley.

"What was that?" I ask her.

She hurries to eat the last bite of her lunch and covers her mouth with her hand when she speaks. "Just helping a girl out."

I glare at her as she stands, swallowing her final bite of her sandwich. "You're not leaving."

"Enjoy your lunch date." She grins and winks at me.

I want to kill her. Luca is cute, he's got dreamy eyes, and a great body, but there is no way I'm his type.

Zero chance.

He could have any girl on this campus, which begs the question, what does he want? It's obviously something. I just haven't figured it out yet.

Luca approaches our table just as Kensley grabs her mess, cleaning it up. "I've got to head out, but my friend doesn't have class for a couple of hours," she says.

Now, I can't even make up an excuse for bailing. I'd give her the finger, but Luca is watching me. And how would I explain that one to him?

His intense gaze never wavers as he studies me. It makes my heart race and my cheeks flush.

I will not catch feelings for him.

"You both should definitely come to the party at our house tonight," Luca says.

Is that why he's stalking me today? He did mention a party he was having, and this isn't the first invite, but I'd like it to be the last. I don't do parties, at least not ones with kegs and athletes, which is likely to lead to bad decisions.

I can't afford any more bad decisions.

"We'll be there. Give Harper the details. I'll catch you later," Kensley says.

The last thing I want to do tonight is attend a party on campus with the hockey team. But my bestie just told Luca Ricci we'd be there.

I glare at her, but the girl is oblivious, or maybe she doesn't care. I love her to death, but that death is seeming to get rather close at the moment.

I don't even say goodbye to Kensley. I'm pissed at her, but I don't think Luca notices. He's too busy staring into my soul. At least it feels that way, intimate, with the way his gaze watches me.

He grabs her abandoned seat, sitting across from me. "It was nice meeting you," he says, but he doesn't even glance in her direction. "See you tonight."

His warm smile could easily be seen as flirtatious, but he's not making eye contact with her. I want to look away. I crave the detachment from the heat building between us. My stomach flips, and I swear the butterflies tremble in my stomach and move lower.

Fuck me.

I will not catch feelings for Luca Ricci.

I chance a glance at my bestie, needing a break from his stare. Kensley grins and waves before jetting out of the deli.

"Friend or roommate?" he asks. He finally glances down at his food, only for a fraction of a second, and I feel as though I can finally breathe again.

"Friend," I say. "My roommate and I don't exactly get along."

He unwraps his sandwich while still giving me his undivided attention. "Let me guess, you're a freshman and got matched with a sophomore who wants nothing to do with you."

"Is it that obvious?"

Luca grins, and those eyes are back on me, making my stomach somersault. "It's the freshman curse. It happens to every freshman who has ever gone to Evergreen. I've been there and, boy, does it suck."

"Any friendly advice?" I ask, glancing at him, hopeful that he can actually help with the Quinn situation. I don't know why I ask, maybe because it's something the two of us actually have in common, aside from Econ 101.

He laughs and shakes his head. His thick hair covers his eyes for a split second before he shakes it away.

"If she's anything like how my roommate was, just steer clear of her," Luca says.

It's no wonder all the girls fall for him; he's got the boyish good looks, charm, and charisma. Not to mention his body. You don't end up as an athlete by sitting on the couch eating potato chips all night.

Why does he have this effect on me?

He's just a boy. Sure, he's easy on the eyes, and that smile warms me to the core, but he's absolutely trouble.

I know it's lust, but how can I lust after someone I barely even know? I don't even particularly like him, but the way my body responds, it's betraying me.

It must be the hormones and the fact it's been a while since I've climbed into a guy's bed.

"What year are you?" I ask. I don't know why, but I had assumed he was a freshman as well, probably because we're both in Econ 101 together, a required class to graduate and, boy, does it suck.

"Sophomore," he says.

"Let me guess, you're the one torturing a freshman this year." He seems like the type who would give someone hell. Probably brags to the team about how pathetic his freshman roommate is this year.

Luca chuckles and shakes his head. "No, I live on campus with a couple of my teammates."

My eyes widen, surprised that he doesn't live in the dorms. Lucky bastard.

"You play hockey," I say, stating the obvious.

I'm pretty sure everyone at Evergreen University knows who Luca Ricci is and that he plays hockey. He's one of their best players. It's pretty common knowledge around campus and in town.

His smile only grows. "You've been to my games?"

I shake my head. "Everyone knows who you are. You're like hockey royalty around here. You get all the girls, probably easy As, too. Am I right?"

"I work for my grades," Luca says, his gaze locked on mine, "but I do okay."

I'm not sure whether his *okay* reference is toward the girls or his grades. Does it matter? I shouldn't care. I don't care. At least, that's what I tell myself.

"Here, give me your phone."

"Excuse me?" I laugh at his boldness.

"I'll text myself, and you'll have my number. Next time this sophomore gives you trouble, let me know."

"I don't need you to fight my battles for me," I say.

Except maybe having him in my corner wouldn't be so bad. He has a lot of clout on campus, and my roommate is boy-crazy. Not that I'd want to set them up. My stomach clenches at the image of the two of them tangling in the sheets.

I'm no longer hungry.

"Give me your phone, Harper," Luca says, his hand outstretched, palm up, waiting for me to deposit it into his palm.

He never uses my first name. I'm surprised that he even knows what it is.

With a resigned sigh, I grab my cell phone from my jacket pocket, unlock it, and hand it to him.

His thumb grazes over my wrist, the slightest caress over bare skin. "Good girl," he says, his eyes on me before glancing down and texting himself from my phone.

His words send a warm hum vibrating through my body. I can't explain the pulsing sensations that his voice elicits with those simple two words and the soft sigh that spills past my lips, unintended.

What the hell was that, and why do I suddenly want to hear him say it again?

TWO

LUCA

I've been trying to get Harper to notice me.

Walking with her after class isn't a coincidence, especially since I'm done until the late afternoon and I either double back to grab lunch or head to my apartment.

She hasn't caught on, at least, and it gives me a few extra minutes with her. Seeing as how we have different social circles, I never run into her outside of economics.

I'm not one to stalk her, but if I had her schedule, I definitely would run into her more often.

Ashton grabs a beer for himself from the fridge. "You want one?" he asks, with the fridge wide open. Guests are pouring into the apartment. There's more than just a few people hanging out tonight.

Ashton Rinaldi is the king of parties. He likes to make everyone feel welcome, and that means inviting everyone he knows and doesn't know as well. I'd be pissed, but he ends up inviting more girls than guys, so it's not usually a bad time. There's always someone available for a hookup.

"I met the perfect girl this morning," Ashton says, popping the top off his beer. "Blonde hair, dark mysterious eyes, rocking body."

"That describes what, fifteen percent of the student population?" I quip.

Ashton rolls his eyes at me. "I didn't catch her name, but I swear I'm going to marry her."

Ashton Rinaldi doesn't seem the marrying type. Probably because he lets all the puck bunnies play with his hockey stick, not all at once. Although he's not opposed to doing that, either, with a couple of the girls. I've heard the sounds coming from his bedroom; it's definitely not a one-on-one situation.

"You've lost your mind," I say, smirking as I take a swig of my beer.

"Yeah, I probably have, but she'd be worth it." Ashton is definitely drunk and maybe a little delusional when it comes to girls. But how could he not be when he sets his sights on someone and never gets turned down?

"And you didn't get her number?" I ask.

"She wouldn't even tell me her name," Ashton grumbles. "But she clearly goes to Evergreen, so I'll run into her." He's confident in his ability to convince any girl to climb into his bed, which isn't hard, since most of the ladies do the chasing.

"Sounds like a massive crush." I chuckle at his discontent. I've never heard him talk about a girl like that, but I'm sure once he beds her, the appeal will wear. It's Ashton. He's the kind of guy who, once you take the toy out of the box, he loses interest in it. He's never bedded the same girl twice.

He snorts. "It's not a crush."

"Right." I shake my head in disbelief. I could give him hell about it for hours, but I'd rather talk to the ladies.

I grab another beer and head through the house, wanting to see if Harper showed up. I doubt this is her scene, but if I'm lucky, her friend will drag her out tonight and I can spend some time outside of class with her.

But realistically, I'm not getting my hopes up.

The girl is way out of my league. She's smart, sophisticated, and I know her type; she doesn't date athletes. The fact that I'm a hockey player works against me. Which makes me like her even more, probably because I have zero chance of hooking up with her.

My stomach sinks the moment I lay eyes on a girl with dark hair pinned against the wall, making out with one of our teammates.

"Oh, hell no!" I hurry across the room and grab Chase Lancaster by the arm and yank him off Nova. The girl is practically a sister to me. She's also seventeen and has no business being at our party.

"What the hell, man?" Chase growls, and I shove him away, knocking him backward several steps, into a flurry of people.

"She's underage," I seethe, and he throws his arms up in the air.

"I didn't know." He glances from me back to Nova. "Seriously?" His eyes rake over her body, wanting confirmation.

She forces a smile, and I swear she's acting out more and more now that I'm no longer living at home. Dressed in a short black leather skirt and crop top, her midriff shows off her pierced navel. There's zero chance her mom and dad know about that piercing.

"Come with me." It's not a question but a command. I grab Nova and drag her upstairs, shoving her into my room. I yank open my closet and grab a sweatshirt off a hanger, tossing it at her. "Put this on."

"You don't get to boss me around like Dad does," Nova scowls, but she catches my sweatshirt in her hands. She doesn't make a move with the article of clothing, holding my stare.

Is she fucking challenging me?

"Do I have to put it on you?" I growl.

Nova is two years younger than I am. We grew up in

the same household. Her father works for my dad, the head of the Italian Mafia.

And like a sibling, my job is to protect her.

"Don't be a dick, Luca." Her eyes narrow. "I was having fun downstairs."

"With Chase?" I choke on her words, coughing, attempting to clear my throat. "He just wants sex, and you're a minor."

"I'm seventeen. He's only a year older, and I'll be eighteen soon."

I refuse to see her point. "No. You shouldn't even be here tonight."

"And why not?" Nova asks.

She finally puts the sweatshirt on over her head, pulling her arms through the sleeves, which at least wins my approval, but I'm not letting her stay.

"Aside from the fact that you're underage and this is a college party?"

Nova shrugs and folds her arms across her chest. "I'll be in college next year. Maybe sooner. I'm graduating a semester early."

I want to be proud of her, but I'm pissed as shit at her showing up and making out with my teammate.

"And next year, you can attend all the parties that you want. I won't stop you."

She snorts. "Yeah, right." A grin forms at the corner of her lips. "You'll be just as controlling as your father. It's in your blood."

"I'm not my father." My jaw clenches and I grind my teeth, seething. My blood runs cold just thinking about the man, Dante Ricci. He's a murderer. A villain. The man who hires people to kill for a living, so that he doesn't have to get his own hands dirty. He uses people like Nova's father for those jobs.

She plays with the hem of the sweatshirt and glances toward the door. "Neither of us want to be our parents. Please, I just need a night away from everything." Her pleading voice is enough to make me give in, because I know all too well what she's going through.

"You're not driving home," I warn her. I know the girl, she'll sneak alcohol, and unless I play babysitter all night, she'll end up toasted. "You'll stay here."

Her eyes light up, and I imagine she's doing a little dance in her head, getting exactly what she wanted. My jaw is tight, and I clear my throat. "You can stay in my room. I'll take the couch."

"You're the best!" Nova squeals, delighted with my offer.

"Next time, call before you just show up." I'm not happy that she's here, but I also don't feel like mingling anymore with the girls downstairs. Besides, I'm not leaving Nova alone tonight, and I don't exactly have a bed for a random hookup, which puts me in a bit of a tight spot.

"I promise," Nova says with a grin and links her pinky with mine.

I grab her arm, hidden behind her back, her fingers crossed. "You're such a brat." Rolling my eyes, I open my bedroom door and gesture for her to head back downstairs.

Heading for the stairs, my gaze locks on Harper as she's standing there talking to Ashton. She glances up at me and bites her bottom lip before excusing herself as she heads for the front door.

I curse under my breath, brushing past Nova.

"What the hell just happened?" I growl at Ashton, grabbing his arm. "I invited Harper tonight. Were you hitting on her?"

Ashton's brow furrows. "What are you talking about? That's the girl I told you about earlier. Hot. Am I right?"

It's not possible.

Ashton's crush cannot be Harper McKenna.

Absolutely not.

Sighing, I shake my head, chasing after Harper. She's already outside, and the air is frigid without a coat or long sleeves, but I don't care. I'd freeze for her.

"Harper, where are you going?" I call after her.

She laughs under her breath, wraps her arms around herself and keeps walking. The street lights illuminate the road as she hurries away from the apartment.

"Away from you," she says a little too loudly.

Maybe she wants me to hear her? "What did I do wrong?" I ask. She's clearly mad. Is it because Ashton was hitting on her, or something else?

Harper stops walking and spins around to face me. It gives me a few seconds to catch up, closing the distance between us. "You really have to ask?" she scoffs at me.

She can barely meet my stare, her gaze everywhere but on me. And I could be wrong, but her eyes almost look like they're glistening, as if she's holding back tears.

I reach out, my fingers guiding her chin up, staring into her dark gaze that captivates me and lures me in. My breath catches in my throat. "You're mad."

"Did you get all that from me leaving the party? You must really be a genius," she seethes.

I bite down on my tongue. She's got a mouth on her. I glance at her lips and then back up to her dark eyes. "Spell it out for me," I say.

Her gaze tightens, and she sucks in a breath. "I shouldn't have to. We're just friends. Barely even that."

She pulls out of my embrace, and the air is even colder than before.

"If we're less than friends, why are you running away?" I ask.

It's obvious she's upset. I'm just not quite sure what I did wrong, and by the look on her face, I'm to blame.

Her tongue darts out, swiping across her top lip. I can't stop myself; I lean in, taking a taste, desiring to silence her anger.

I expect her to pull away, to smack me across the face, yell, scream. I'm waiting for her reaction, but it isn't what I'm anticipating.

Her lips melt into mine, and she leans closer, her fingers trembling against my chest as I wrap my arms around her waist, pulling her tighter. The kiss starts out simple yet passionate, but when she doesn't back off, I drag my tongue across her bottom lip.

Her mouth parts, granting me entrance as I deepen the kiss, and I hear the perfect sweet moan fall from the back of her throat that elicits a primal response deep within me.

Fuck, she sounds hot.

I want to hear her moan my name, listen to her panting and breathless as I bury my cock deep inside of her.

Harper pulls back, breathless.

Her cheeks are rosy and her lips swollen. She's a gorgeous sight, and the cold air surrounds me yet again. I'd forgotten I was freezing while kissing her.

"We can't," Harper says and pulls her hands back from my chest. "I'm not *that* girl."

My gaze tightens. "What does that mean?" I've never been more confused in my life.

"I know what you were doing, Luca. I'm not an idiot. You're not bedding two girls in one night. Well, not me."

Harper turns and keeps walking, heading down the road, leaving me standing there dumbfounded.

Bedding two girls? Who the hell does she think I slept with?

And then my mind flashes back to Nova, walking with her down the stairs, her wearing my sweatshirt. Does she think I slept with *her*?

THREE

HARPER

I kissed Luca Ricci; what the hell was I thinking?

Okay, I wasn't thinking. I let myself experience the moment a little too much, and I'm regretting it.

Not the kiss.

I definitely do not regret kissing Luca.

What I regret is the fact that he had just hooked up with another girl—she definitely looked like a freshman—and then he chased after me.

Who does that?

The most eligible bachelor, who happens to play hockey for Evergreen University. It doesn't hurt that he's easy on the eyes. I'm pretty sure he has a fan club who chases after him at hockey games, screaming his name and cheering him on.

She's probably part of that stupid club.

At least that's what I imagine happens after games.

I've never been to any of Evergreen's hockey games, and I don't plan on attending one in the future, either.

I'm not into sports. I'd rather stay in the dorm reading a book until the early hours of the morning.

After what happened this evening, I am never going to a hockey game, ever.

And then there is Ashton Rinaldi, who I ran into on my way to class and again at the party. He kept chatting me up when I wanted to find Luca.

I hate parties. I only showed up tonight because Kensley insisted that I attend.

And then there was a small part of me wanting to show up for Luca.

Which is asinine. Why did I think the invitation meant anything?

He probably invites every girl he's friendly with, and I'm sure there is a long list since he's an athlete.

Showing up and getting stopped in the foyer to talk to Ashton wasn't bad, it just wasn't what I wanted. I didn't show up tonight to party.

Stupid of me, I know. I showed up at a party, not to party. Don't ask. I didn't say my decisions made sense.

I showed up to see Luca.

The party was at his apartment, and I was a little more than curious to see his place. Not that I expected the grand tour or anything, but I was hoping to spend a few minutes with him.

Ever since he showed up at lunch, I can't get him out of my head.

Stupid hormones.

I'm probably reading too much into his friendliness. I tend to do that, think that a guy who is being approachable actually likes me.

I just have to keep reminding myself that he's friendly with all the girls at school. I'm nothing special.

Besides, I'm not even looking for a relationship right now.

My studies take priority, it's why I'm here; I'm on a scholarship and need to keep my grades up. I cannot fuck this up.

Ashton steals my attention, keeps me from wandering off as he keeps talking to me, making jokes; clearly, he's interested.

He's nice enough, but I don't date athletes, and I'm pretty sure he'd be more interested in a one-night stand than anything long term.

Not that it matters, because I don't have those feelings toward him, the ones that give me butterflies or make me feel like I'm floating on air.

That's how I'm beginning to feel around Luca.

I'm not sure when it happened. Sometime between us grabbing a bite together and seeing him walk downstairs with another girl, my stomach tangled into a knot and all I felt was devastation, hurt, anger, and so I ran.

I didn't expect him to chase after me or kiss me into silence.

Staring up at the ceiling of my dorm room, I lie on my mattress, contemplating everything I could have done differently, and I grab my phone, cursing under my breath.

Kensley.

I left her at the party and didn't even say goodbye. I shoot her a quick text, letting her know I went back to the dorm.

Ten seconds later, my phone rings.

"You bailed on me?" Kensley asks, and I can hear the pulse pounding beat through the phone. She's still at the party, but it's more muted than one might expect, like she's locked herself in a closet or bedroom to chat with me.

"Long story," I say with a sigh, not wanting to elaborate.

"You should come back out. Luca seems pretty down, and I'll bet you might be able to cheer him up."

I scoff at her suggestion. "Plenty of other girls for that, like the one he hooked up with earlier."

Silence fills the space, although it's more like muffled music blaring through the phone. "I'll come over," Kensley says.

"Don't." I hesitate but know it's better if she stays out and has fun. "It's late. Enjoy the party. I'm just going to get some sleep."

"I'm sorry."

"What?" I ask. Why is she apologizing? It isn't her fault in what happened tonight. "It's fine."

There's commotion in the background, and then I hear his voice, the one that sends tingles right into my stomach. "Can we talk?" Luca asks, his voice soft, warm, inviting.

"There's nothing to talk about," I snap hastily. "I'm hanging up now."

"Wait!"

Luca manages to grab my attention, and I pause, letting silence envelop us.

"Are you still there?" he asks when I haven't spoken a word for several long, drawn-out seconds.

"Regrettably, I haven't hung up yet."

"Can you let me explain? The girl who you saw me with earlier—"

"You don't owe me an explanation. You're free to hook up with whomever you want," I say.

Just because he invited me to the party doesn't mean he was asking me on a date. He was just being friendly, suggesting that I come to the event.

"She's practically a sister to me. We grew up in the same house. Nothing happened between us upstairs. I gave her a sweatshirt because I didn't like what she was wearing."

"Wow," I say. "Judgmental much?"

"She's seventeen! I don't need the guys drooling over her. She's like my little sister."

I sit up in bed, pulling my legs to my chest. "Seventeen? What's she doing at the party?"

"Long story," Luca says, and this time, I do feel like he's avoiding telling me everything.

The jealousy that courses through my veins seems to dissipate. He doesn't owe me an explanation. "Okay, I'll see you in class. Bye, Luca." I end the call and toss my phone onto the mattress. I'm not in the least bit tired, but continuing that phone call seemed like a bad idea.

We're just friends. Barely even that, and we kissed. It's no big deal. It's not as though I haven't kissed other guys before. But with Luca, it feels different.

———

I head outside, down the stairs of the dorm, and feel his eyes on me. Luca.

I walk past him, not wanting to assume anything. He could be standing here, waiting for anyone.

"I wanted to walk you to class," Luca says.

"You came all the way down here to walk me to class?" I ask.

"How do you know I wasn't already at the dorms?"

I bite my tongue. I don't know what he was doing or who he was doing it with. "Were you?" I raise an inquisitive eyebrow as I head toward the sidewalk. I'm not sure I even want to hear his answer.

He follows beside me. "No," he says and laughs.

He almost sounds nervous, confessing the truth to me.

I glance at him as we walk before returning my attention to the sidewalk in front of me. It's chilly outside, but at least the snow has mostly melted by Monday.

"Do anything fun over the weekend? Aside from attending the party?" he asks, his attention completely on me.

His stare is overwhelming, and my breath catches in my throat. "Yeah, I had a date last night."

It's a lie. I spent the afternoon hanging out with Kensley, and then we watched movies until I left for bed.

His jaw twitches, and he forces a smile.

"Anyone from the party?" There's an obvious sense of discomfort in his question, like he's curious but not sure he can handle the answer.

"I don't kiss and tell," I say with a smirk. We stand at the corner of the street, waiting for the light to change.

He shifts on his feet and shoves his hands into his coat pockets. "Please tell me it's not Ashton."

I clear my throat and turn to face him. "Excuse me?"

"Listen, I know I can't tell who you can and can't date, but Ashton—"

"You're right. You can't," I say, hurrying across the street.

I head into the building, but instead of wandering into the classroom, I slip into the bathroom, giving myself a few minutes to chill out. Besides, if Luca gets to class first, he'll be forced to take a seat, and then I can sit somewhere else, far away from him. Otherwise, he'll sit next to me, like he always does.

At least that's my plan, but when I head out of the bathroom, he's standing by the door, leaning against the wall, and hasn't gone into the auditorium yet.

"Stalking me?" I ask.

A sly smile crosses his face. "Would I do that?"

I may not know Luca very well, but it's obvious to me that he's trouble. The jealous vibe about Ashton is a major red flag, and I should stay far away from him.

But he pushes himself off the wall and strolls right toward me. He fears nothing, least of all rejection.

Me?

I fear him. Not in the aggressive, he'll hurt me type way. No, I fear that I'll fall for him, and he'll break my heart. It's not like it hasn't happened before. I've been in love once, and picking up the pieces of my shattered heart was one of the hardest lessons I've had to deal with in my past.

"Yeah, you definitely seem the stalkerish type," I chide and brush past him for the classroom.

He grabs my arm, spinning me back around to face him. Our bodies brush against one another as he's stepped closer, invading my personal space.

My breath catches in my throat as I stare up into his heated gaze, the butterflies returning all at once, making my lips dry.

"Not a stalker," he says and shakes his head, his gaze

unwavering. "I just happen to know what I want. Who I want."

And my breath hitches as I swear the air is stolen from my lungs. He's mesmerizing to stare at, the faint smile playing at the corner of his lips, the dimple on his right cheek as he studies me.

"We have to get to class," I whisper, and he gives a brief nod before releasing me from his grasp.

A slight whimper escapes the back of my throat, a moan that I'm not even sure where it came from, and I swear I hope that he didn't hear it.

But he did.

He raises an eyebrow, and I just want to disappear into oblivion. There's no ignoring the emotion that he elicits, and he's grinning at me like the Cheshire Cat.

When the hell did I start crushing on Luca Ricci?

FOUR

LUCA

That sweet, delicious sound that Harper makes fills me with a thousand fantasies, all involving her naked and moaning my name.

I follow her into Econ 101, which is the most boring class this semester, but somehow, I'm enjoying it far more than I should. It doesn't hurt, the view of her ass with her walking in front of me. If only it were warmer outside, and she didn't have a thick jacket covering her assets.

I snag the seat next to her as she blatantly attempts to ignore me. She retrieves her laptop from her bag, her attention straight ahead as if I don't exist.

But I'm confident that she feels my presence as much as I crave hers.

And I fully intend to make up for the disaster of a party she attended because I know girls like Harper, and she'll never want to attend another one.

The girl is a bit of an open book, and while I love a little mystery, it helps that I can read her, probably better than she knows herself. The fact that she's trying to avoid me, but the tinge of her cheeks and her stare keep telling me she's inwardly fighting her feelings, denying herself the pleasure that comes with liking me.

Yes, I'm confident she has feelings for me.

Just about every girl at Evergreen has a crush on me. That sounds egocentric, but it's true. It comes with the territory of being a star athlete for the university. I get tons of girls chasing after me, puck bunnies, as we call them.

But it's the girls who don't do the chasing that I'm drawn toward, girls like Harper McKenna.

Perhaps I like a bit of the chase, trying to win her over, and Harper isn't an easy girl to win the affection of. She's closed off, and as much as I know her type, there's still so much that I don't know about her.

I barely pay attention because I took economics in high school and it was a breeze. This class isn't much different for me, and since our homework assignments are always online, I don't worry about actually listening to the professor.

My focus is spent on watching Harper.

She's typing away at the keyboard, trying to write everything down at once, but it seems to me like she's not catching the bigger points and just trying to remember everything.

I could help her with that, *studying*.

We have a test next week, which doesn't worry me too much, but it's the perfect excuse to spend time together. "We should get together and study for the exam," I say.

"Why, so you can borrow my notes? Take your own, Ricci."

I tap my head. "I've got it all up in here."

She glares at me, unconvinced.

Not a complete surprise, since I did ask her to send me her notes the first few weeks of class. I was trying to find a reason to talk to her early on, and she kept shooting me down.

Class is dismissed, and Harper closes her laptop and shoves it back into her bag. She doesn't answer me.

I saw her grade on the last assignment. It wasn't great. She could use my help, and she knows it.

Harper lets out a soft sigh. "Just studying," she says, glancing at me. "I need to ace my next exam to bring up my overall grade."

"I promise, if you study with me, I'll make sure you get an A." It's not a promise that I should make, but economics has been a breeze, and I'm sure I can help her with her next exam.

Her gaze tightens before she relents. "Where should we meet up, the library?" Harper asks.

"Come by my place. My roommates will be out of the house. We can study in the lounge."

She stares at me like I just suggested we go skinny-dipping in a frozen lake.

"I promise, no funny business, just studying," I reiterate.

"Okay," she relents and follows me out of the classroom. "Can you do later this afternoon or tomorrow?"

"Any time after three today."

We settle on four o'clock, which sounds perfect because it'll put her over my place into the early evening hours, and I can suggest dinner afterward. "Do you remember my address?" I ask, making sure that she doesn't have an excuse for not showing up.

"It's only been a couple of days," Harper says. "I'll catch you later." She heads out the door, and I follow her, walking her to her next class. I'm not letting her get rid of me that easily. Besides, with guys like Ashton on campus, I don't want to be fighting for her attention.

"I'll walk with you," I say, accompanying her outside.

She presses her lips together and smiles. "You don't have to. I know you don't have a class this direction."

"What makes you so sure about that?" There's no way that she knows I've been walking her to class and then doubling back to head to my place. I've been careful, waiting until she's inside and out of sight before turning around. The last thing in the world that I want is for her to think that I'm desperate and trying too hard.

"I saw you the other day, walking back," she says and points in the opposite direction.

"Oh, that's because I forgot my phone in the classroom." The lie comes out quicker than I intend. It flows naturally, a protective mechanism of sorts.

Her eyes squint, and she nods. "Okay."

Does she believe me? I'll have to be more careful.

"It's okay if you walk me to class," Harper says, and her nose wrinkles. "It would actually be kind of sweet."

"You can't go telling your friends. I have a reputation to uphold," I say, nudging her as we walk alongside one another.

"A reputation, huh?" She bites her bottom lip, and my cock stirs in my pants. There's something sinfully hot about her mouth, the way her tongue darts out after chewing on her bottom lip, and I imagine her warm lips on my shaft.

Fuck.

Inwardly, I groan.

Thankfully, she isn't the wiser.

————

I have never felt quite so nervous in my life, and all this pent-up energy for a study date. It's because I'm spending it with Harper. And the studying part is just a formality.

If I had suggested that she come over and hook up, there was zero chance that she'd have said yes. Even if I'd offered to hang out and watch a movie, I'm pretty sure that she'd have come up with an excuse.

I've cleaned my room twice. I tidied up the place, in case she wants to see my bedroom upstairs. I'm hoping Ashton comes home early and Harper suggests studying someplace quieter. And that someplace isn't on campus, like the library.

It's like I'm a teenage boy all over again, my heart

racing and my stomach tangled in knots, when I hear a soft rap at the front door.

I hurry to the door. Right now, no one else is here. Ashton is at class, and Liam is barely ever home. He has a twin sister, Sophia, who comes and goes like she lives with us. She doesn't attend Evergreen, but she does attend our parties and hangs out after our hockey games.

She's off-limits, since she's Liam's sister, and all the guys on the team know not to date her. He's made it clear that anyone who touches her will be subjected to his wrath.

And Liam's got quite a temper. No one even thinks twice about hitting on Sophia, and it's not because she isn't gorgeous. Our teammates are afraid of Liam and that he might chop off their dick if they so much as hit on his sister.

Liam doesn't know that I slept with Sophia. We both agreed it was a one-off situation and that it would never happen again. Plus, she's afraid if Liam finds out, she won't be able to hang out and party at our place.

I'm more concerned that Liam might murder me in my sleep. It's best if he doesn't find out.

Sophia has just as much to lose if her brother finds out, so we both have a reason to keep it a secret.

"Hey, Harper," I say with an eager smile as I open the door.

"Hey." She hurries inside, shivering. As she steps out of her shoes and removes her coat, I try not to let my gaze wander over her body, but it's impossible.

She's wearing a deep burgundy sweater that goes down to her knees and black leggings that hug her thighs. Her sweater accentuates every delectable curve on her body.

It's hard not to stare.

Harper presses her lips together, and her eyes shine with mirth. "Are you ready to get started?"

I lead her into our study lounge and grab a seat on the sofa, leaving her room to join me. There's a table situated in front of us, and I've already got my books stacked up along with some notes I printed off from our online portal for class.

"I wouldn't have agreed to study with you, but I saw your score on our last exam," Harper says, and her cheeks redden. "You're pulling an A in the class, aren't you?"

I laugh under my breath. "You noticed that?"

"What do you get out of studying with me?" she asks, sitting next to me on the sofa. She unzips her backpack and retrieves her textbook and laptop.

"Aside from enjoying your company?"

That catches her attention, and she glances up at me, raising an eyebrow. "You didn't ask me to study so that you'd flirt with me the entire time, did you?"

"Maybe?" I laugh and realize if I lie, I'll only bury myself deeper. I don't want to chance her standing up to leave. "I saw how you did on the last exam and thought you might want a little help. And the benefit for me is that I do like spending time with you."

Her gaze tightens as she stares at me.

"I didn't come over to hook up or whatever."

I smile. "I didn't think I'd be getting lucky." A guy can fantasize, but that's all it would be, at least for now. I need to give her time to realize how much she wants and needs me. "Just let me do this for you, Harper."

She emits a soft sigh and nods. "Okay, yeah, sure."

We open our textbooks, and I go over her notes with her and explain the equations and concepts that she's been struggling with for the past couple of weeks. After a solid hour of going over everything, she sits back and stares up at the ceiling.

"Is your brain fried?" I tease, sensing that it might be a little too much for one day. I wasn't planning on doing a cramming session with her, but that's about how it's going.

"No, it's just—you're so much better of a teacher than our professor."

I nudge her playfully. "I'm not sure that says much. It's not like I pay attention in class. Well, not to the teacher."

Harper grins. "I knew you were staring at me!" She glares at me playfully, and her cheeks are bright red.

Is she embarrassed or turned on? I've dated girls like Harper. Jumping in headfirst and being overly direct just pushes them away faster.

"Would I do that?" I laugh, feigning ignorance when she playfully smacks me on the arm.

"Yes, I think you would."

I shrug with a smile. "Maybe." That's all I'm giving her. Not because I don't want to be direct and scream to the world that I like her, but because that type of intensity would scare her away.

And she's all I think about all the damn time.

I'm not sure when it even happened, when desire and lust turned to want and need. But I'd do anything to make Harper McKenna happy, and if that starts with helping her pull up her grade in economics, so be it.

We spend another hour going over what will be on the exam before I hear her stomach grumble. I'm growing hungry, as well, but I don't want to chance the night will be over the minute I suggest dinner.

"I should probably go, eat." Harper leans back and stretches.

Everything about her is both adorable and sexy. Her messy hair, her rosy cheeks. The soft breaths that escape her gorgeous swollen lips that beg to be kissed.

It takes everything inside of me not to lean over and run my fingers through her hair and steal a taste.

"I'll order food," I say, hoping the invitation isn't too forward for her. "We can finish studying while it gets here."

"Okay, but my treat, since you're helping me more than I'm helping you," Harper says.

There's zero chance that I'm letting her pay for dinner. "What do you feel like eating?" I ask.

"What do *you* feel like eating?" she counters back. Harper runs her fingers through her long tresses, and damn, is it hot. I love that messy hair look on her.

"I asked first," I say, suppressing a growl and the need to claim her, to tell her she's what I want to devour. If I let my mouth run, she'd tear out of the place and never speak to me again.

"You can't go wrong with pizza," she suggests.

We agree on the toppings and where to place the order. She shoves her credit card at me, but I refuse to take it while I'm on the phone, turning my back on her. I retrieve my card from my wallet and read off the digits, finalizing the order before hanging up. "Forty-five minutes."

"You said I could pay," she huffs at me.

A smirk plays on my lips. "You can pay for the next date."

"Oh no, this isn't a date." Harper's eyes widen, and she gestures between us, shaking her head adamantly. "And who said anything about us doing this again?"

"Oh, come on. We're only halfway through the semester. Admit it, you're going to need my help for our final."

She curses under her breath. Harper has to know that I'm right, but she doesn't seem like the type to easily admit defeat. "Fine, but next time we order takeout, I'm calling it in." Her eyes are blazing, and I like how easy it is to rile her up.

"Sure, sure." I lean back on the couch, laughing.

Harper presses her lips together, her gaze tight as she stares at me. "I should just give you cash for the pizza." She reaches for her backpack on the floor.

I grab her wrist, stopping her. "I'm not taking your money."

"And why not?" she asks, tilting her head, staring at me with wide, doe-like eyes.

Her stare is invigorating. So is her tenacity. I release my grip on her wrist, and I swear I hear her whimper.

Fuck, this girl knows how to get to me.

FIVE

HARPER

Luca is far more charming than I first anticipated. I shouldn't be surprised since he gets all the girls he could want. He's certainly had plenty of practice flirting his way into their beds.

That's one of the perks of being an athlete. I'm not blind to it. There are tons of girls who stare at him in class or "accidentally" knock into him to win his attention.

And he always falls for it, bending down, helping the girl pick up her books that she dropped.

You'd think that half the freshman class at Evergreen

are clumsy, based on how many times he runs into a girl on a weekly basis.

Or maybe Luca is clumsy.

Not a chance in hell is he the one bumping into them. He's got finesse on and off the ice.

I'm pretty good at ignoring it. In the beginning, I honestly didn't care, but the more time I spend with Luca, the more I want to chase the other ladies away before they even have time to make eye contact with him.

Do I feel the embers of jealousy tingle and burn my flesh? Maybe a little.

We've spent the past several nights studying together. Mostly, it's Luca teaching me everything that I didn't grasp in class, which feels like a lot.

The first night, we had the place entirely to ourselves. Tonight, Ashton is in the living room with a movie, and the girl who had been upstairs at the party with Luca is crashing on the couch.

"Do we have to watch another boring documentary?" she asks, although it's more of a whine.

"Nova, you decided to hang out with us. And I enjoy watching this shit," Ashton says.

Luca chuckles and shakes his head, smiling at me. We're situated at the kitchen table, with him seated beside me, studying. He leans in, his breath caressing my cheek. "Ashton can't stand documentaries. He's just torturing Nova for showing up uninvited."

I don't quite get the relationship between all of them. "Is Nova his girlfriend?" I ask. It's impossible to ignore them in the next room over, the open layout not offering much privacy.

"Definitely not. She's seventeen. I'll kill him if he lays a finger on her."

I press my lips together, wanting to ask but not sure I should. "Why is she hanging out on campus?"

"Home life is complicated," Luca says, not further elaborating.

I've always been close with my family, but I had friends growing up who preferred my parents to their own. I get the explanation, but it also feels like an excuse.

My mind is miles away from the book staring open at me on the table. "Do you want to take a break?" I suggest and nod toward the living room.

"And watch that garbage?" Luca asks, raising an eyebrow. "I'd rather study," he says, making eye contact with me.

That's what we've been doing, studying, for the past two or so hours. I refrain from glancing at my watch. I don't want Luca to think that I'm ready to leave, because that's the furthest thing on my mind.

He's quiet for a moment, scoots his chair back and stands. "I get it. You need a brain break." He heads for the fridge.

I watch him from across the kitchen. He's tantalizing and hard to tear my gaze away from.

"You're staring," Luca says, before glancing over his shoulder at me.

How the hell did he know that before turning around? Was he guessing that I was watching him because that's what all the other girls do when he invites them over to study?

"Do you have a lot of study dates?" I ask and immediately regret my question. I'm not sure I want to know the answer.

He grabs two bottles of water from the fridge and the bag of potato chips sitting on the counter, bringing the snacks back for us to consume. "That's funny," Luca says, offering me the water. He drops the open bag of chips on the table between us.

I can't help but stare up at him peculiarly. "What?"

"You thinking I have time to tutor other girls." He smiles warmly and plops himself back down beside me. "We can order dinner, but it'll probably be a while until it gets delivered. I thought you might want something to snack on in the meantime."

"I have dinner plans for tonight, but thanks." I grab a potato chip from the bag and stare at Luca. It's hard to imagine him without a long line of girls waiting to be *tutored*.

"Hot date?"

There's a hint of jealousy in his tone.

The truth is that I have zero plans, but I don't want Luca to think that I have no life.

I smile coyly and glance at my watch. "I should start packing up and head out." I organize what I can and shove the rest into my backpack.

"Let me drive you home."

"It's only a couple of blocks, I can walk."

"It's dark out already. You're not walking alone," Luca says with insistence.

I don't argue, mostly because it's chilly outside, and while there isn't any fresh snow on the pavement, there's plenty of ice from the previous week. "Thanks."

Standing, Luca grabs my backpack before I can toss it over my shoulder. He's got it tight in his grip. The chair squeaks across the kitchen floor, announcing our departure.

"Are you leaving already?" Ashton asks from the couch. He pauses the documentary, and there's an obvious sigh from Nova, seated beside him.

"Please don't leave." Nova's eyes plead with me to stay as she shuffles around on the sofa and clasps her hands together. "I'm begging you, if it's me with these two monsters, there is zero chance of watching anything enjoyable tonight."

"Drama queen much?" Luca asks, tilting his head slightly at Nova, as if he's warning her to behave.

"Only because you're a remote-control *hog*!" She grabs the pillow that was left out for her to crash on the couch and throws it at Luca.

The pillow lands with a soft plop onto the wooden floorboards.

"I can't remember the last time someone cleaned that floor," Ashton says, grinning at Luca.

"That's because you can't be bothered to clean anything, ever," Luca says.

Nova's face scrunches up in disgust. "Gross!" She hops off the couch and grabs the pillow, an unsatisfied look on her face as she attempts to dust off the pillowcase. Groaning under her breath, she glances up at me, looking for someone to come to her aid.

There's a teasing sibling energy between them that I can't believe I didn't see earlier.

"Nova, do you want to grab dinner while these two boys clean their apartment?" I ask.

Luca lifts his right hand a few inches, gesturing at the backpack in his grip. "I thought you had a hot date tonight." He glances briefly at Ashton, and there's a look between them that I can't quite distinguish.

"I said I had dinner plans. You inferred *hot date* from that," I say.

Luca turns his full attention back to me. "With your friend, Kensley?"

I could make plans with Kensley, and I might catch up with her in the dorm, but she wasn't my dinner plans. I emit a soft sigh, lick the corner of my lips because, suddenly, I feel like I've been caught mid-lie. "Okay, fine. I don't have dinner plans with anyone. Happy?" My tone comes out snippier than I intend. Luca hasn't done anything wrong, it's just my defenses coming up, trying to keep my heart from getting stomped on all over again.

His shoulders seem to relax at my admission. Is he happy that I don't have plans? He grabs my coat and helps me into it, like a perfect gentleman, before tugging me closer, pulling at the lapels. "You need to button this monstrosity up. It's freezing outside, and we don't want you to catch a cold."

His breath tickles my cheek. His hands firm and strong, keeping me close, sends tingles throughout my entire body. My breath catches in my throat, my eyes slightly glaze over while I stare at him, perplexed.

His fingers deftly button my jacket for me when I don't move quickly enough to do it myself.

I laugh, surprised by his actions.

"What's so funny?" Luca asks, working on the buttons from the bottom of my coat. He's on the fourth one already.

"I've never had anyone button my coat for me."

"Never?" he asks. "Not even when you were a kid?"

I gently brush his hands away, doing the remaining buttons on my jacket myself. "Maybe when I was a child. I don't really remember anyone doing it for me. It's been a long time."

"I'll bet that's not the only thing that's been a long time," he mutters under his breath playfully.

I laugh, shocked by what I'm hearing. "Excuse me?" My mouth hangs open, staring at him, perplexed. I secure the last button near the top of my coat, dig my hands into my pockets for my leather gloves, and playfully slap him with one of them on his arm before shoving the gloves back into my coat pocket.

"What exactly are you implying, Ricci?" I say, using his last name, scowling playfully at him. I'm not angry, just shocked by his comment.

"That it's probably been quite some time since anyone laced up your boots for you too," he says with a smirk. "What did you think I meant, McKenna?" he teases, using my own last name but in a much flirtier way.

I step into my boots, lean down and zip up the side, which makes it so I don't have to lace up my heavy winter boots. It saves time, and right now, I'm ever so grateful not to be fumbling with the laces.

Luca slips his shoes on first and then grabs his winter coat. I swear he had me putting everything on backward just to fluster me. Is everything a game to him?

"We're heading out now. Let's go," Luca says. He grabs his hat from his jacket pocket, slips the beanie on over his head and glances back over his shoulder at his roommate. "Clean the damn place while we're gone."

Ashton tosses up his middle finger at Luca, who waves and salutes his teammate on the way to the front door.

Nova throws the pillow at Ashton and hurries around the sofa, grabbing her jacket and slipping into her shoes. "Wait for me!"

Luca leans in, his breath teasing my ear as he whispers, "Did you really have to invite my sister on our first date?"

My heart palpitates, and I suck in a nervous breath. It takes every bit of energy not to react to his words *first date*. If I pretend that I didn't hear him, maybe it'll make the encounter a thousand times less awkward.

"Cute coat," I say to Nova, smiling brightly as I pull my own beanie on to keep warm.

"Thanks," Nova says. She walks beside me as we head outside, Luca right behind us, grumbling under his breath about being the third wheel.

I spin around on my heels, stopping, and he nearly collides with me. "What was that?" I ask, feigning innocence, all smiles.

He looks flustered that I spoke up, or maybe he didn't realize I could hear him. He's cute but not nearly as quiet as he thinks he is.

He jingles his keys at me. "Are we taking my car, or walking somewhere in this frigid weather for dinner?"

It's not much of a question. It's too cold to walk anywhere. We pile into his vehicle. I sit up front in the passenger side while Nova is seated in back. The car hums to life, but none of us has decided where to go eat. The heat blasts cold air, which doesn't help.

"Where are we going?" Luca asks. He glances at me and then, presumably in the rearview at Nova.

"I don't know," Nova says. "I don't know what's around here."

Luca shifts, glancing at me. "What do you feel like?"

"Not freezing to death," I joke. "How about the Chinese buffet around the corner?" It's cheap, has decent food and, more important, is close to campus.

Nova chats the entire drive over to the restaurant. The car doesn't even have time to heat up before he parks out front.

I climb out of the car, and Luca hurries to open the front door as we step into the warmth of the building. He brushes against me. "Chinese food for our first date, huh?" he teases into my ear.

I can't even say it wasn't my idea because it was, but also, no one else was making a decision. They both left it up to me. "This isn't a date," I whisper a little too loudly, and Nova glances over her shoulder at us.

"Oh gosh, did I invite myself along when I shouldn't have?" Nova quips.

Luca and I both answer in unison, but he shouts, "yes," and I answer with a resounding, "no."

"I've only ever seen you studying with Luca," Nova says, clearly changing the subject. She doesn't offer to leave, and I'm grateful. I'd also be worried if she tried to wander back to the house in the cold dark of night.

We grab a booth, Nova sitting on one side, and I climb into the opposite, which apparently gives Luca the opportunity to slide in right beside me. Maybe I should have opted to sit next to Nova, but I suppose if he doesn't try any funny business, it'll be all right.

"You don't go to any of the boys' hockey games?" Nova asks.

I shake my head. "I've never been to a hockey game."

"Never? You've watched a game on television, though, right?" His eyes are wide, like I might have just traumatized the poor guy. Maybe he's beginning to realize that it could never work between us.

"Never," I say and shrug. "I'm not really into sports. Sorry." I offer a faint smile, meeting his intense stare.

"No sports at all? What about the Olympics?"

That wins a smile. "I watch some of the Olympics when it's on, but that doesn't count."

"What about the Super Bowl or the Stanley Cup Playoffs?"

"Boring."

"Would you ever attend one of my games?" Luca asks.

I inhale sharply. It hadn't even crossed my mind. "You want me to watch you get your butt kicked by a bunch of guys?" I smile, trying to lighten the mood. "I suppose I could be down for that. Will there be popcorn?"

"I like her," Nova says, grinning at Luca. "Can we keep her?"

I snort with laughter and then cover my face with my hand, humiliated.

"Oh, that's adorable," Luca says, nudging me. "Don't be embarrassed."

We give the waitress our drink orders and then migrate to the buffet before coming back to take a seat at the booth. Luca is still grabbing food while Nova and I have a minute of girl time alone to chat.

"What's the deal with your brother?"

"What do you mean?" Nova asks.

"He's a cute guy, clearly has the girls pining for him. What's his deal?"

"Oh!" Nova's eyes widen. "Do you mean, does he have a girlfriend? No, I don't think so. It's been a while since I've seen him hook up with anyone."

"A while," I repeat, taking a slow bite of food, trying to digest her words.

How long is a while? A week, a month? Is it just a dry spell for him?

Luca brings his plate heaping with food to the table and slides into the booth beside me. "What are we ladies talking about?" he asks, smiling at the two of us.

"Harper was just asking about your deal."

"My deal?" Luca says, nodding slowly, eyes raised, like he's getting all the secrets of the universe from his sister. He shifts and stares at me. "You could have just asked me directly. My deal is I'm single, for now."

He grabs his fork and digs into his dinner, leaving me staring at him and speechless.

He's not hitting on me. He's flirty, jokes about dating me, but doesn't actually ask me out. Not that I necessarily want him to ask me out, only because I can already see how this won't work out between us. We live in completely different worlds. He's a jock, I'm a bookworm. We don't even share the same interests.

Oh, the over-analyzing is tiring. I shove my fork into my food and take a bite, keeping me from saying anything that will embarrass me further.

"I like her," Nova says, nodding at me, as if I'm not right there and can hear every word.

"Me too," Luca chimes in.

"Wow, I have a fan club," I joke, trying to break the awkwardness that I feel with the two of them discussing me, right in front of me.

"Sign me up," Luca says. "Do I get a card that I can carry in my wallet?"

"Sure, if you've got twenty bucks." I hold out my hand teasingly.

———

After dinner, Luca drives me back to my dorm.

He leaves the car running, with Nova in the backseat, but climbs out when I get out.

"Are you walking me to the front door?" I'm half-joking but also kind of hopeful.

Although I don't know what I'm hoping for exactly. Another heated kiss? When I think about that night, my lips still tingle and warmth floods me.

"Is that okay?" Luca asks as he grabs my backpack from the trunk and slings it over his shoulder.

"Sure, I guess that's fine."

"What kind of gentleman would I be if I didn't make sure you made it home safely?"

I don't want to admit that I'm not ready to go home. If Quinn, my roommate, is around, it'll just be hell until bed. I suppose I'll pop on some headphones and watch a movie on the laptop until I fall asleep.

"I could never deny a gentleman anything," I joke.

"Is that so?" he grins, and I feel heat flame my cheeks.

I head for the dormitory door, and he's right beside me. We enter together, Luca escorting me inside the building and all the way to the front door of my dorm.

"Have a good night, Harper," Luca says, and he leans in, brushing his lips chastely over my cheek. I turn slightly, letting his lips brush mine, needing a taste, wanting a reminder of what I felt that other night.

It all comes flooding back and more, the heat, the tingles pooling in my stomach and lower, making me feel things new and foreign. The butterflies are back, but this time I'm not upset or angry. I know he's not interested in another girl, at least not Nova.

A part of me wants to invite him inside my dorm room, to finish our exploration and discover so much more about each other. But I know Nova is in the back of the vehicle, the heat on, but she's waiting for him to return, to take her back to the house. And it's that tiny voice, the annoying one that stops me from taking things any further.

Even though I want it.

I want him. I want Luca Ricci.

It's fact. I'm falling for him, and I don't know how to stop or even if I want to.

"Goodnight," he says again, this time softer and sexier as his lips pull away. He's smiling, his eyes dark and shining down at me.

I refrain from dragging him into the dorm room. I'll have dreams about it, fantasies for the next several nights, imagining how it would go down if I tugged on his shirt and pulled him into the room with me, our limbs tangling together between the bedsheets, naked, hot, and sweaty.

A soft sigh escapes my lips, heavy and throaty as I whisper, "Goodnight," back to him.

He plants one more kiss on my lips and waits for me as I fumble with my key before slipping into the dorm room, closing the door behind myself.

The warmth, the heat that flowed through me, instantly chills when I hear the sound of Quinn laughing and moaning as she's making out with another random guy on her bed.

"I'm home," I say, in case she didn't see my presence or hear me enter.

She huffs, but it's not sexy in the slightest. It's clearly annoyance with me interrupting her. "You again," she mutters.

"Yeah, me again." I've tried giving the sophomore her space, been polite, even tried being cordial, but I'm done making friends with a girl who wants nothing to do with me. It's my room, too, and just because she has a guy over doesn't mean I have to be hanging out in the hallway, again, until she's done.

"Can't you, like, get out for a while? Give us some privacy."

"How about you go back to his place?" I say and jab my thumb toward the door. I reach for my headphones, already knowing she has zero desire to leave.

My phone buzzes with a text; it's an unfamiliar number. I open the message, seeing it's from Nova and it's an invitation to a party next weekend. I don't respond right away. I barely know the girl, and I'm not really into the party scene.

Of course, attending the party means that I'll have a chance to see Luca again, which just makes me feel even more conflicted. I have feelings for him; they're obviously growing into something that I'd rather not experience, considering who he is—one of Evergreen's top hockey players.

Why should that matter? Because he can get any girl he wants, and though he might think he wants me, I'm not sure if he does. Because he'll grow bored and tired with me if that's the case. We have nothing in common.

I hate sports.

He lives and breathes hockey.

His friends are all hockey players. It's his life. His father is probably a huge hockey fan and got him interested in the sport.

My phone buzzes again, another text message.

Nova: Luca won't be at the party. We're celebrating my 18th birthday, girls-only sleepover. I hope that's not a problem.

Harper: I'll be there.

I barely know the girl, but she's practically a sister to Luca and I don't have many friends on campus.

Although technically, Nova doesn't even go to this school.

I exhale and shut my eyes, rubbing at my temples.

Spending time with Nova is a far better option that hanging out with Quinn. Not that my roommate and I ever hang out together. If being forced to share a room counts, that's the most we've done.

———

I ace my Econ exam thanks to Luca spending hours with me, explaining everything better than our professor. He's walking me to my next class, a faint smile on his lips, like he's got something exciting to share.

"You're happy," I say, glancing at him. Is it because the weekend is almost here? I'm looking forward to not having classes for two days. "Any special reason?" I ask. He seems almost gleeful.

"Just glad you passed your exam."

It feels like it's more than that, but I don't push. "I suppose it's because I have a good teacher."

"You'd better mean me," Luca says, nudging me as we walk together outside. "Are you free tomorrow to hang out?"

"I can't. I have plans. Nova invited me to her birthday party on Friday night. Do you have any gift suggestions?"

"Aside from not going?" Luca mutters, his brow furrowing and his nostrils flaring.

I stop walking and turn to face him. "Are you two not getting along?" It's only been a couple of days since the three of us hung out, but maybe something happened between them.

He scratches the back of his neck. It's an awkward gesture, and he seems uncomfortable answering. "I just think you'd have more fun here on campus this weekend."

"I already told her I'm going. I'm not going to disappoint her." Besides, it's not as though I have other plans, and it'd be good to get some time away from Quinn.

"You do know it's a sleepover, with a bunch of high school girls."

"You make it sound scandalous. She's turning eighteen. I'm eighteen," I say, gesturing at myself. "There won't even be any boys staying over, so if you're worried about her, relax."

"Relax," he grumbles through gritted teeth.

I've clearly hit a nerve. I'm just not sure which one or why.

I turn on my heels and pick up my pace, needing to get to class. Luca hurries to follow me. "I can't convince you not to go?"

"I don't see the problem," I say.

He doesn't answer me. Whatever problem he's concocted has stayed buried within him.

We approach the building, and I reach for the doorknob, glancing back over my shoulder at Luca. "Maybe we can hang out on Sunday."

"Yeah, maybe." He's somber, the sparkle in his gray-blue eyes gone. "I have a practice game with the guys on Sunday, but maybe we can work something out."

"Catch you later," I say, heading into the building for my next class.

———

I don't hear from Luca again. I'm not sure why I'm expecting to see him or hear from him. It's not like we're dating.

And yet it feels different.

Almost like he's upset with me because I'm going to Nova's party. Maybe I'm reading too much into the situation, but it was evident that he didn't want me to go.

I swing by the local bookshop and pick up a gift card as a present. I don't know what she likes to read or really anything about her. Luca was zero help when I asked him.

I put it in a cute little bag along with a stuffed animal of a narwhal that caught my eye. Luca's team is the Narwhals, so maybe that'll win me some brownie points. Does Nova even like hockey?

Sitting on my bed, I tuck everything nicely into the bag and add a little glittery tissue paper to hide the surprises nestled inside, when the dorm room door swings open.

Quinn is back, and for the first time, she's not tied to the hip of some new guy. She is, however, wearing a jersey for Evergreen's hockey team.

And not just any random jersey, it's got the name Ricci on the back and his number 21. The numbers are hand-stitched, and clearly, it was custom-made.

I'm both mad and jealous at the same time.

Although I'd deny it if anyone asked.

"I'll be out of your hair tonight," Quinn says. She opens her closet, grabs a few things, including some blue and white face paint and hair clips. "Going to see the Narwhals play tonight. I can't believe I managed to snag close-up seats to see Luca Ricci play! He's so hot."

My stomach does somersaults when she says *his* name.

I shouldn't care. I don't like hockey, and I sure as hell don't like Quinn. But the thought of her cheering for Luca makes me nauseous. Does that make me a terrible person? I should be happy that he has fans, but the mere fact that it's Quinn is bothering me.

"Are you going to be sleeping here tonight? Because if I can get ahold of that hottie hockey player, I'm going to make my move and score with him." She winks at me.

Bile rises in my throat.

"I'll be gone tomorrow night." I don't know why I even tell her.

"Oh. Boo," she pouts. "I always have to be so accommodating for you." She's laying it on thick, whining and trying to get me to feel bad for her. "Why can't you just do me this one solid and find somewhere else to sleep tonight?" She's got the doe-like eyes which may work on the boys but do nothing for me.

I scoff at her words. "Why can't you keep your legs closed for one night or fuck him in the locker room?"

Her eyebrows rise. She seems surprised that I responded. The whiny, coy attitude has vanished from her demeanor. "Not a bad idea," she says with a smirk.

I hate myself for even suggesting it. I wait for her to leave before grabbing my phone and texting Kensley, telling her I need her to come over pronto.

Within ten minutes, she's in my dorm room, sitting across from me on the bed. "Spill the tea," she says.

I wasn't exactly forthcoming via text. I just messaged her to get her butt over here because I was freaking out.

"Luca is playing tonight."

Kensley purses her lips together. "Yeah, I know. But you don't like hockey."

"Quinn apparently does. The girl was fawning all over Luca. You should have seen her custom jersey."

"So, she's wearing a jersey with his name on it. Big deal. What's got you so worked up?" Kensley is waiting for me to elaborate.

"She wants to sleep with Luca, has her sights set on him. If you know anything about Quinn, she'll get her claws into him, and he won't even see it coming."

Kensley stands, stretching her legs and her back. She heads for the door.

"Where are you going?" I ask.

"If you're this hung up on Luca, then we need to get there first."

"And say what?" I shake my head; we can't do that. I'm not going to fight for Luca or make him choose between Quinn and me. I'd never win.

Kensley is laughing and grabs my hands, pulling me up from the mattress. "We're going to watch him play, cheer for him, and clearly catch his eye. Quinn doesn't stand a chance if you're there."

"That's funny," I say, pointing at Kensley.

"What?"

"You thinking I have half a chance with Luca. We're just friends."

She rolls her eyes, unconvinced. Kensley shoves her phone into her pocket and turns slightly, glancing over her shoulder at me. "Grab your school ID."

"This is absolutely crazy. It's never going to work," I say. "We're just friends."

"I know, you keep repeating that phrase, but I swear it's because you're trying to convince yourself that you don't have feelings for him." She guides me across campus, toward the arena. I've never stepped foot inside, but she leads me around inside like a pro.

"Are you secretly a hockey fan?" I whisper into her ear as we're ushered to our seats before the game starts.

"I wouldn't call myself a hockey fan; I don't own any jerseys or merchandise, but I've been to a few games growing up. My little brother loves hockey."

"Does he play?"

"My parents would never let him get on the ice, it's too dangerous."

"Helicopter parents?"

"They have their reasons," she says, without further elaborating.

Our team, the Narwhals, come out and start skating around the ice, doing warmups. I catch sight of Luca, skating on the ice, stretching, getting ready for the game.

"Ricci!" Quinn squeals, jumping up and down in the front row behind the plastic paneling, in an attempt to garner his attention.

He looks up, smiles, and nods before skating off.

I can't stop watching Quinn, like a trainwreck that needs further investigating.

Kensley elbows me. "Quit being jealous of her."

I grumble under my breath.

"What's that?" Kensley asks, she's not one to ignore anything or let it go.

"I'm not jealous of her."

Kensley stands in front of her seat. "Good, because you don't have any reason to be," she says.

I glance at her, unsure of what she means by that remark. I eventually get up when three students try to walk past us, but there isn't quite enough room in the row. The stands are starting to get more crowded and filled in.

"You're looking at me like I'm the devil," she says.

I laugh, but it's forced. "I'm not."

"Okay, be jealous," Kensley says with a shrug. "You're just hurting yourself. You know he likes you. Quinn will probably throw herself at him because that's what she does."

I groan. That's precisely what I'm worried about. Quinn doing just that, and then Luca falling hook, line, and sinker for her because he's a decent guy.

"I just don't want to see him getting his heart broken."

"I'd be more worried about her breaking his dick."

A snort slips past my lips. "That is not a visual I need."

Kensley cackles and nudges me. "Relax. Luca is going to be stoked when he sees you at his game."

"He's not going to notice me." I'm merely a tiny dot in a sea of blue and white.

"If you say so."

The guys seated next to us are wearing jerseys. In fact, nearly everyone in the stands is wearing a jersey or, at the very least, the team colors. Kensley is dressed in a black sweater, she practically melts into the audience. Me, on the other hand, I'm wearing bright pink.

I stick out obnoxiously, but it's not likely Luca is looking in the audience. Why would he?

My gaze catches sight of him skating on the ice, and I swear he lays eyes on me. It has to be my imagination because I see him crack a grin.

Doubtful.

He's probably thrilled with the turnout for tonight's game, or maybe one of his teammates made a joke. It's not like he's alone on the ice. His buddies are with him, waiting for the game to start.

Luca waves in my direction, and I glance around the crowd, assuming he's just waving at everyone, saying hello. He is friendly, I mean, he always has been with me. He's friendly with the girls in class and around campus who literally walk into him to get him to notice them.

While I've never known him to be overly social, he does have a lot of friends, and he gets along with his roommates.

I wouldn't know what that's like.

Now, that's something I'm jealous of and willing to admit.

Quinn. She's just an annoying distraction.

And that's when I see her standing in the front row behind the plexiglass, waving at him and making a heart symbol with her hands.

I can't watch anymore. I plop down onto my seat and let the crowd surround me, hide me, from having to witness Quinn flirting with Luca.

What was I thinking coming here tonight with Kensley? I can't watch Quinn flirt with *him*.

"What's wrong?" Kensley takes her seat beside me.

I want to tell her to *read the room,* but she's probably not watching Quinn like I've been, feeling the jealousy stir within me, the anger bubbling to the surface. Why does she have to go after Luca? She could have any guy in the school. Why *him*?

The crowd begins to sit, and while it's not exactly quiet, the players begin disappearing off the ice. "Where are they going?" I ask Kensley.

"Locker room, most likely. They'll announce the team and players as they come out onto the ice."

"Harper!" Luca shouts at me, waving frantically before his hockey buddies drag him off the ice before the game.

Quinn turns around, scowling and scanning the crowd. I slink behind the tall guy seated in front of me, hiding from both Luca and Quinn, although mostly from Quinn. Not that Luca didn't completely embarrass me.

Why was he shouting my name?

SIX

LUCA

My eyes aren't playing tricks on me. No, it's definitely Harper McKenna in the stands, watching the team warm up before our game.

Ashton grabs my jersey when I ignore him, dragging me off the ice before we get in trouble.

"Did you see her?" I can't believe Harper showed up, *Little Miss I Hate Sports.*

"Who, Harper?" Ashton is shaking his head as we head down the hallway. "No, but I heard you scream her name like a maniac. You're embarrassing yourself over a girl."

"Shut up." I body check him as we step into the locker room.

Ashton rolls his eyes, laughing. "Too bad we like the same girl."

My stomach plummets at his words. "You like Harper?"

I knew he had a little crush, but I thought he was over it.

His dark eyes glimmer as he offers a rare smile. "Don't worry, I know better than to steal what's yours."

She isn't technically *mine*. Although I want her to be. But if Ashton knows to keep away from her, perfect.

"Good."

"Find out for me if she has a sister," Ashton says with a wicked grin.

I'm not doing Ashton's bidding for him. If he wants a girlfriend, he can find one for himself. "Ask her yourself next time she's over."

"Or I could ask her out myself," he taunts.

I lunge at him, and several of our teammates hold me back from lashing out physically.

"Save it for the ice, Ricci!" Coach shouts at me.

I know Coach is right. I shouldn't be fighting with Ashton, but it's hard to let that shit slide, especially when he's talking about *her*.

Harper may not be my girlfriend, yet, but I don't want anyone else even thinking about dating her.

Because the truth is that I do want her. I'm more than just slightly interested. And the mere thought of anyone else putting their hands on her sickens me.

The rage that builds inside of me, I hate it. The feeling of agony, this tight ball that is nestled in my chest, falling into my stomach with every deep breath that I take. I'm drowning. The more I think about anyone else so much as paying attention to her.

I'm a walking red flag, I know. I blame my father for that, and as much as I don't want to be him—I despise the man—I also grew up under his roof. It's naïve to think I could be anything else.

Which is why I'm here playing hockey. The one sport he absolutely despises. He thinks I'm weak and foolish for not following in his footsteps. He wants me to run the empire one day.

No fucking way.

I don't care if he offered me a million dollars, I'm not doing it.

I know too much about the mafia, the family, the business that the men do, and I wish I didn't know any of it.

I wish I'd never walked in on my father murdering an innocent man in the basement of our house as a child. Some things haunt me still to this day, and I refuse to so much as handle a gun. The smell of gunpowder makes my stomach roil.

I'm sure that Dante, my father, looks down on me for not joining him in the business. In fact, it's a truth that I know. He's told me as much, and yet, it makes no difference to me.

I avoid going home. The moment I was accepted to Evergreen University, I hightailed it out of that miserable place of existence.

I heard Mom crying when I got accepted on a full scholarship. She's the only reason that I'd consider going back home, but I can't, and I won't.

My heart hammers in my chest with the sound of the crowd cheering and shouting. The announcer riles up the audience and begins introductions for our team as we head back onto the ice. I search out in the stands for Harper. There's a sea of teal and black for the Narwhals, our team, but she's hard to spot at the moment, and she was wearing bright pink.

The crowd is on its feet, cheering for us, which feels amazing. I love home games.

Did Harper leave already? She made it crystal clear that she hates sports. Fifteen minutes of watching us working out, getting ready to play, and she already bailed.

———

We get our asses kicked. It's brutal, and it is partially my fault. I'm not playing my best after spotting *her* in the stands, and Ashton riling me up about asking her out.

Distracted is an understatement, because I kept glancing up, looking for her. I got my face planted into the glass several times, the puck stolen from me, and my ass kicked even more.

Harper was nowhere to be seen.

Sure, there are tons of people in the stadium. It's crowded, and she probably is just buried behind someone taller than her. Doesn't make it any easier for me, knowing she's out there watching my annihilation.

Or worse, she was watching, and then after I shouted her name and waved at her, she was embarrassed and left.

That thought nagged at me the entire game.

So much so that I couldn't focus on the stupid puck sliding across the ice or the opposing team rushing for it. I didn't give the game the same energy that I usually do. It's like my heart just isn't in it, because my focus is on the wrong thing.

After the game, Coach notices, pulls me aside and reams me for a good ten-minute tongue lashing.

He's pissed because I fucked up, royally.

I have nothing to say. I don't even attempt to make excuses because I know he's right, and that's the only thing that hits harder. I sucked because I was distracted by a girl.

Fuck me.

I need to get Harper out of my thoughts. She's dangerous.

I shower in the locker room, and Ashton glares at me when I'm drying off. "What?" I ask. It's impossible to ignore his angry stare. It's like heat radiating off the asphalt.

"You played worth shit tonight."

"Thanks," I mutter and slip on my clean clothes. "Appreciate that, *pal.*"

"I'm not your personal ass-licker." He stares at me, his gaze never wavering.

I hadn't expected him to know what I meant, and it makes me feel even more like shit. "Sorry," I apologize.

Ashton watches me with a quiet intensity while I lace up my tennis shoes and clean up my locker.

Usually, I'd snap back at him, ask him what he's staring at, but after the night I had, I'm done. If he has something to say, he'll come out with it. I know him well enough to know he won't hold back.

I'm not disappointed.

"Catch feelings for the cute blonde?" He doesn't have to say her name. He sees her all the time at the house, the two of us studying together.

I bite my tongue to keep from answering. A little pain actually feels good right now. I deserve it after how shitty I played tonight.

"Damn, you don't even deny it," Ashton says with a chuckle. "I knew it! Those study sessions are a lot more interesting than you let on."

I roll my eyes, grab my phone and keys and head out of the locker room, making my way through the building and toward the exit for my car.

Ashton is right on my heels and riding my nerves as he hurries to keep up with me. "You're still driving me home tonight, right?"

I ought to let the bastard walk home, but I'm feeling generous. He scored two goals. I let the other team sink one in. I shove open the doors to the stadium and feel a blast of icy cold air hit my skin.

It's freezing outside, and quite a walk to the car. I can practically see my breath, and I fiddle with my keys in my pocket. "Get in, but don't make me wait for your ass," I warn him.

Ashton hurries, knowing that I just might leave him. I'm in that kind of a mood tonight.

What I don't expect is to see a strange girl leaning on the driver's side of my car. She's wearing my jersey along with a pair of black leggings. She's shivering and has her arms folded across her chest, but I can't imagine it's doing much to keep her warm.

"Can I help you?" My tone is sharp, quick, and with as much bite as the cold nipping at my fingers.

I don't recognize her, and if she's a puck bunny, I'm not interested.

Her cheeks are rosy, and I can't tell if it's the chill outside or my harsh tongue that has her blushing.

By now, most of the cars have left the lot, which made it fairly easy to find my vehicle buried near the back, and with no one parked on either side of us anymore, it's not as though she's having trouble finding her vehicle.

"We have Chemistry," she says, whispering at me, her eyes heavily caked with eyeliner and mascara. Her eyes are mesmerizing, and I inhale sharply, trying to remember her. "I was hoping I might buy you a drink," she whispers, keeping her voice low and sultry.

She's pretty, but I'm getting weird stalker vibes, considering she's asking me out in front of my vehicle. How did she know which car was mine in the lot? "I'm flattered but not interested," I say. I can't recall her name, and while I am taking Chemistry 201, I swear I've never noticed this girl before.

She probably wasn't wearing my jersey in class though, either.

"Are you going to give her a ride?" Ashton asks, yanking the car door open and climbing into the passenger side. He slams the door shut before I even have time to answer him.

The blonde pouts and shivers again, but this time it's much more noticeable. I can't help but wonder if it's intentional, like she's trying to tell me with her body language she's cold. Which I don't doubt, considering her attire.

"Could you give me a ride?" she asks, her blue eyes staring up and hopeful. "I don't live far. I'm in the dorms."

I glance back over my shoulder. There's no sign of Harper, the one girl I want to see tonight. I guess she bailed out early or left with her friends since I doubt she showed up alone to watch the hockey game.

I sigh and reluctantly open the back door. "Climb in. I'll drop you off."

"Thank you!" The girl squeals with delight and climbs into the backseat. "I'm Quinn," she says, quick to introduce herself.

I shut the door and hurry into the driver's seat, turning on the engine to warm up the vehicle.

"I'm betting you already know our names," I say. She's wearing my jersey, which looks handmade.

"Luca Ricci and Ashton Rinaldi," she says. "Hard not to know who the two of you are, since you're Evergreen's best hockey players on the team."

The girl knows how to stroke an ego.

"I'm better," Ashton quips and turns around, flashing Quinn a megawatt smile. "You're wearing the wrong jersey, Quinn. This guy, he spends more time in the penalty box than on the ice." He jabs a thumb in my direction.

Usually, I'd argue who's the better player, which, of course, is me, but I'm not feeling it tonight. My thoughts drift back to Harper, seeing her earlier in the stands. I can't stop thinking about it.

Why has she gotten under my skin?

"So, that game tonight. Tough," Quinn says. She's fueled with excitement and energy, neither of which I'm feeling at the moment. After a game, I'm typically soaring on the endorphins.

Tonight was a hard loss. A wake-up call that I need to get my shit together for our next game. I have to deal with Harper, whatever that means ... I'm not even sure.

I drive over toward the quad and glance up at Harper's building. "Give me a minute. I want to catch up with someone," I say to Ashton.

"Really? You're going to do this now?" Ashton huffs

and leans his head back on the headrest. "Just leave the engine running, would you?"

I leave the engine on and hurry outside in the chilly air. "I'm in Building B," Quinn says.

Harper lives in Building B also.

"That's where I'm heading," I say. I follow her inside, and since it's late, she uses her ID pass to gain access to the building. She lets me enter with her, allowing me to bypass security, and we head east into the building for the elevators together.

"Which floor?" Quinn asks as I follow her into the elevator.

"Eight."

She presses the button on the eighth floor and leans against the elevator wall. "Thanks for the ride back home," Quinn says. "If you ever want to grab that drink." The smile never leaves her face, her sapphire eyes shine as she stares up at me, hopeful that I'll say yes.

"Appreciated, but I'm busy." I don't want to hurt her feelings, but I have zero interest in getting to know this girl. She's pretty, seems nice enough, but there's something about her that feels off.

It could be the fact that she was waiting for me at my car tonight after the game.

Major red flag.

It doesn't take a genius to see that one staring you in the face.

The elevator dings, and I gesture for her to step out first. I follow behind her, and we head in the same direction.

Quinn has a light bounce in her step, almost like she's giddy from tonight. Although I'm not sure why. That girl is a mystery, one I don't need to involve myself in any part of with her. "Are you sure I can't offer you that drink?" She glances at me over her shoulder with a knowing smile.

Does she think that I came up here for her?

I thought I made it clear that I wanted to visit with a friend.

"That was sweet of you, trying to protect my reputation from your friend. But I'm not an innocent little girl, Luca. I can take care of myself."

What is she talking about?

Quinn fiddles with her key in her hand and stops in front of 802, the same room that I'm heading for to visit Harper. She shoves the key into the lock and glances at me once more before yanking on my jersey, pulling me closer, and landing her lips on mine forcefully.

SEVEN

HARPER

I've been stewing since the moment I left the arena, angry at Luca for embarrassing me and even more perturbed at Quinn for trying to steal Luca's attention.

Practically wearing a hole through the rug in the dorm, I've been waiting for Quinn to come home. There's no way that she got her wish and hooked up with Luca.

It's obvious she wants him, and Quinn gets everything she wants. Every single time.

It's nauseating.

I hear her key in the lock, but when she doesn't open the door, I yank it open, wondering what the hell is taking her so long. I shouldn't want her to come home, but now that I know she's outside, it's like a ticking time bomb and I'm waiting to explode.

I've never hated anyone more in my life.

Scratch that.

My eyes burn as I catch sight of Harper locking lips with someone in the hallway. They break apart, probably coming up to catch air, and my heart shatters into a million pieces and I slam the door shut.

"Harper!" Luca shouts to me, and tears threaten my eyes.

I refuse to cry.

There's nowhere to run. The bathroom is in the hallway, and I grab my headphones and shove them over my ears. It's what Quinn wants, isn't it?

I close my eyes, crank up the volume as I listen to my angry metal playlist and shove a pillow over my head, trying to suffocate myself.

Why do I always have to catch feelings for the wrong guy?

There are muffled voices, my bed dips and I'm about to scream at Quinn and Luca when I pull the pillow from my face and open my eyes, staring up at Luca.

He gestures to the headphones I'm wearing, and I reluctantly remove them. I inhale sharply, praying my face isn't red from the few tears that threatened to fall.

"What?" My question is sharp and filled with torment.

"I came over hoping we could talk."

I laugh darkly, feeling a twisted knot inside my stomach. "Talk?" I repeat. "It's hard to imagine us doing that with you shoving your tongue down Quinn's throat."

He sighs and glares at Quinn before returning his stare to me. "That's not what happened."

"You came up to her room with her. Let me guess, you gave her a ride after the game too?"

Silence falls between us.

"You're jealous," he says, a realization seeming to dawn on him, and all it does is make me feel even more uncomfortable.

"I'm not. I don't know what you're talking about." I sit up in bed, toss my legs over the side of the mattress. "There's no reason for me to be jealous," I say, stating the obvious.

I pretend to be miffed by his accusation, although he might be on to something. However, I refuse to confess as much to him.

"You're crazy, and why did you come over to talk?" I ask as I try turning the line of questioning onto him.

He should be the one being interrogated for having a lip-lock session with my roommate.

"How long have the two of you—" I gesture between them, hoping this isn't an actual *thing,* because I could not deal with knowing they were hooking up in our dorm room.

"I've been pining over him for weeks," Quinn says, her voice dripping like honey, sweet, sugary, and full of desire.

"There's nothing between her and me," Luca states, pointing at Quinn. He doesn't say her name. I'm not sure he even knows it, but that wouldn't be a terrible surprise. Quinn does like to bed any guy with a pulse, and I doubt she knows the names of all the men she's hooked up with, either.

"Except for tonight," Quinn coos, and my stomach somersaults. I shuffle on my feet, waiting for someone to elaborate and hoping that it comes from Luca.

"I gave you a ride home, not my first regret of the evening," Luca says. His phone starts buzzing in his pocket, and he curses under his breath. "I left Ashton waiting in the car."

Quinn smiles, but the sweet, coy act she had going falls away. "Invite him up. We could make it a *real* party."

Luca scoffs. "That's not happening. Harper, can we talk?"

"You should go downstairs; you can't make Ashton wait forever," I say. I don't want him to leave, but I also don't want to have a conversation with Quinn in the room, either.

He reaches toward me, brushing a strand of hair out of my face and behind my ear. His touch is warm and sends tingles coursing through me. I lean into his touch, staring up at him. I want to kiss him and scream at him, both simultaneously.

Is it normal to get this worked up over a guy?

"You're probably right," he whispers, but he doesn't move. "This weekend, you, me, a quiet night someplace romantic. An actual date," he says, making his intentions crystal clear.

His fingers are like a warm current, offering my body a taste of what's to come. The back of his fingers graze my cheek, and I exhale softly, grateful that I'm seated, or I would most certainly have wobbly knees.

How does he exert this type of power over me?

It's just a crush. The words bounce around in my head, but he's too easy to fall for, and I'm trying not to get swept off my feet.

"I like you, Harper, in case you haven't noticed." He's laying his cards out there, in case him telling me he wants an actual date isn't enough. "I want the opportunity to get to know you better."

I lean into his touch as his fingers caress down my jaw.

I want to kiss him so badly, but I'm holding back. He just kissed Quinn.

And maybe if I'm being honest with myself, I'm a little worried I'll taste her if I kiss him. And if I don't taste her cherry lip gloss, then what happens if I fall for him even faster?

That can't happen.

I have to keep things slow, cautious.

Because it's Luca Ricci.

He's hot.

Smart.

Athletic.

And, more importantly, has all the girls fawning over him. I don't want to be another number on his roll call.

It's more than that—so much more that I can't even deal with again.

"So, how about that weekend date, just the two of us? Or we could make it the entire weekend," Luca says and grins.

I give him credit for his persistence. "Do you mean our first date with your little sister hanging around doesn't count?" I'm teasing him about Nova because maybe it'll break the thick sexual tension hanging in the air.

"Definitely doesn't count." He offers a wry smile. "So, Saturday or Sunday? Pick your poison," he jokes.

Can I trust him with my heart?

I can't erase the image of her lips on *his*, but I believe Luca, that she threw herself at him. That sounds exactly like Quinn.

I like Luca, a lot, but trusting him is something that doesn't come naturally for me. I've been burned before, with my high school boyfriend. He swore he loved me, that we'd go to Evergreen University together, and that he only had eyes for me. That I was the center of his world.

It was all a line of absolute crap. I caught him in bed with two cheerleaders, and then he had the audacity to invite me to join them!

That memory boils my blood and haunts me to this day.

Yes, I have trust issues. That jackass was the reason for them, and while I know not every guy is a complete douchebag, he was on the football team. Which makes me want to steer clear of jocks.

And Luca plays hockey. It's hard not to see the similarities. He has girls throwing themselves at him constantly. It's a lot to compete against, and well, I worry that, in the end, I won't win. I'll end up with my heart crushed again.

Luca will inevitably find someone else who doesn't have trust issues, who is more fun to be around and who actually likes sports.

We have nothing in common. That hasn't changed, and it never will.

My heart flutters as I stare into those cool gray eyes that give me swarms of butterflies in my stomach.

What's the harm in one date?

"Sunday," I say. We had talked about going out on Sunday earlier in the week; the plan still stands. "I'm seeing Nova for her birthday party this weekend, but

I'll be home Sunday for a date. I might be home late Saturday since the party is Friday night, but I'm not sure what time." I stand, gently pushing him toward the door, an errant smile forming at the corners of my lips. Just thinking about a date with him has put me in a better mood.

I'm feeling cautiously optimistic.

"You're going over to my house?" he asks, his voice catching in his throat as I practically push him out the door.

"Yeah, Nova's birthday. Remember?" I smile faintly as I gesture for him to get going. "Ashton is waiting for you."

His phone buzzes again, as if on cue.

"Right," Luca says and sighs. He looks perplexed. I'm not sure why.

"Goodnight, Luca," I say and close the door behind him. I spin around on my heels, glaring at Quinn. If looks could kill, I'd be cleaning up a dead body right now.

EIGHT

LUCA

It'd be impossible for me to forget Nova's birthday. Especially since she's been raving about it for the past week.

Is she excited?

Yes.

I think it has more to do with her becoming an adult than anything else. She's been yammering on about colleges and how she's been accepted into Evergreen University next semester.

I can't say I'm surprised, given the fact that she's on campus all the fricking time. It's a good thing we get along, or I'd be shoving her out the door and tattling on her for showing up.

There's no way Moreno and Paige know she spends so much time here. There's zero chance they'd want her hanging around other college-aged boys.

As far as they know, she's never been on a date.

I know better.

Nova can keep a secret.

Turns out, so can I.

Truth is, I get along better with Moreno than my own father, which doesn't say much, considering Moreno isn't the least bit friendly or warm. I suppose that's what you get when you house the mafia together under one roof and then try to raise a family.

The answer: fucked-up kids.

I've avoided going home. At any opportunity, I've stayed on campus, but Nova is having her eighteenth birthday party at the house and hearing Harper tell me she's going, all I can think is *this is a bad idea.*

I've tried texting Nova and suggesting she change the location. She can crash here for her birthday, let the girls spend the night on the living room floor or couch.

The response I got was a crying laughing emoji.

Nova is as stubborn as her father.

Which means I'm packing a bag for the weekend before driving home, the one place I swore I wouldn't return to, no matter what.

Ashton knocks on the open bedroom door as I stuff the last of a few items into my duffel bag. "You ready?" he asks.

He's not from the area. He grew up in Chicago, part of an extension of the family if you will, not blood but brothers, nevertheless. Mafia is always family, either they love you or they kill you.

Turns out, our families get along well enough not to kill one another. It helps that we grew up in different parts of the country. There aren't territorial disagreements between brothers.

"Yeah, let's go." I'm not thrilled with traveling back to the compound where I grew up, but Nova is having her party, and the truth is Harper is going to be there, and someone has to keep an eye on her.

———

We make our way to the compound, and Ashton is quiet. He's been here once before, when we were just kids. It was the first time we met. I wonder if he even remembers it; we were little.

I don't see Nova's car outside, and I'm not sure how Harper intends to get here. I probably should have offered her a ride, but it's not like I want to encourage her to come to Nova's party.

I'm fine with Nova and Harper hanging out. It's great they're becoming friends. What isn't so hot is visiting this place with Harper.

She doesn't have the slightest clue about our family, and I don't intend to tell her that my father runs the mafia. There's no reason for her to know the kind of man he is, how he orders his men to kill his enemies and steal from them. He's not a good guy.

Mom goes along with it only because she swears her family is no better, which is saying something. I've never met them.

Hard to believe she came from an opposing mafia family, but I've done a little research and investigating when I was in middle school, and she's not lying. I thought maybe Dad had all of them killed, but they're still around, causing mayhem and murders of their own.

"Looks like we're here early," Ashton says, noticing the same thing that I do; Nova's car isn't outside, and the front entrance is pretty sparce. If she were having friends over, I'd expect a few more vehicles out front.

We park the car, and I hesitate, tempted to turn around. "What time does the party start?" I ask.

Ashton shrugs and climbs out of the vehicle, not the least bit bothered by our early arrival. He grabs his backpack from the backseat along with an overnight bag.

I grab my duffel from the backseat and lug it over my shoulder. While I don't want to stay over, I also know if Harper is intending on spending the night, I have to be here and make sure she's safe.

Tonight will be chilly, which gives me an idea and also a reason to keep her out of the house as much as I can.

I stalk around back. Ashton hurries after me, bags in hand, as if I'm walking to a back entrance to enter the house. He's going to be in for a treat, because the least amount of time I can spend around my father is my plan.

If I'm lucky, he's out on business this afternoon and tonight as well.

Don't imagine I'll actually get lucky.

I toss my duffel onto the back porch. I'll deal with it later, when I'm forced to go inside the house.

There are a few stray branches, broken and lying on the ground. I gather them and keep looking for more.

"Put your bags by the door and help me," I say, heading for the tree line and the forest that wraps around the property. There's fencing that keeps the lot secure, but the forest expands far and wide.

"Help you?" Ashton mutters under his breath. "What are you doing?"

"We're going to build a bonfire," I say, carrying a decent stack of branches and tossing it into the stone fire pit in the backyard. I head for the forest, grabbing any wood that's broken and dried to keep the fire roaring. I'm going to need a lot to keep the girls outside, especially since it's going to be chilly.

Ashton picks up a stick and points it at me. "You know how to build a fire?"

"Mom had me join the Boy Scouts when I was a kid. She thought it would help me if I ever got lost in the woods."

Ashton grabs another branch from the ground. "And your father?"

I inhale sharply, not wanting to think about *him*. "He—"

"You're home," Dante says, stepping out onto the back porch, squinting from the sunlight as he stares at me. "And you've brought company."

It's about as warm a welcome as I'd expect from him. He's never been overly affectionate as far as I remember. Hard to be when you're in charge of ordering men to kill for you.

"Hi, Mr. Ricci. I hope it's okay that I came by unannounced," Ashton says rather quickly, the words almost slur together, and I swear I can hear his heart race from across the lawn.

I suppose he knows a bit about having a don as a father, since Aurelio runs the Chicago mafia. Although Ashton and his father get along, they at least talk to each other on the phone once a month.

My father never calls me.

But if he did, I also wouldn't answer it.

"You're home!" My mother's voice carries across the grounds, her excitement bubbling over as she hurries outside barefoot to greet me. "You didn't tell me you were coming, but it is Nova's birthday," she says more to herself than to me.

She embraces me in a hug, and for a second, I wonder if she'll ever let go. "It's good to see you and Ashton," she says, glancing at my friend.

Mom met Ashton again when we were moving into the apartments on campus. She offered to come help us move out of the dorms, and while I didn't take her up on the offer, she still showed up to help. Which meant her mostly shuffling a couple of boxes between places for us.

"Thanks, I was just setting up a bonfire for tonight," I say, gesturing to the pile of sticks and branches haphazardly thrown into the fire pit.

"Perfect night for a bonfire," she says. "I'll have the guys bring out enough chairs and make sure there's ingredients for s'mores."

Ashton's eyes light up. "Gosh, I haven't had those since I was a kid."

Mom smiles and glances at me. "Should I have them pick up anything else at the store?"

"You'd have to ask Nova," I say. "It's her party."

She laughs and nods. "I'll follow up with Paige and see if she needs anything."

Paige is Nova's mom and my aunt. We grew up in the same household, under the same roof. One big, not so happy family.

"It's good to see you. How's school?" Mom asks. She waits a beat before Dante wanders back inside. "I came by this week and watched the Narwhals."

"You didn't," I say, my stomach plummeting. She saw me play worth shit. Wonderful. "Was Dante there?"

"Your father couldn't make it," Mom says. "He had other pressing matters to attend to. You know I really hate that you call him that."

"It's his name, isn't it?" I point out.

Mom nods and shakes her head, defeated. "Yeah, I just wish the two of you could get along."

"Maybe if he wasn't a murderer—" I don't say anything further because I catch sight of Harper walking up the long driveway in a bright red dress. "If you'll excuse me," I say and brush past her, not finishing our conversation.

"Luca," Mom calls after me, but I ignore her as I hurry to catch up with Harper before she makes her way to the front entrance and chances running into Dante.

I jog across the lawn, ensuring that I catch up with her. The cold sting feels surprisingly good. "Harper!"

Her eyes widen, and a faint smile plays on her lips. She's carrying a gift bag in one hand and a small overnight bag on her shoulder. "Let me help you with that," I say, taking the heavier of the two items, slinging the bag over my arm.

"Thanks. I didn't expect to see you here tonight," Harper says. "I thought you might have practice or something."

I wince, wondering if she's referring to the shitty game we played last week.

"Wouldn't miss Nova's birthday party."

"Even though she said it's an all-girl's sleepover and no boys are allowed?" Harper quips. She's smiling, and I half-imagine she's teasing me.

"Well, we're like family, and this was my house growing up." I point at the compound, which resembles a mansion. I haven't stepped foot inside yet, and I'm waiting until the last possible moment when I have to go in. Maybe I can convince the girls to camp outside tonight, and I can watch their tent, make sure they're safe.

"Wow," Harper says, taking it all in. "It's gorgeous. What does your family do for a living?"

The million-dollar question.

"Best you don't ask that around here," I whisper, nudging her as I lead her toward the backyard.

She sighs, and her heels sink into the soft grass. I grab her elbow, keeping her steady. Her legs are bare, the dress just above her knees. She's got to be freezing. She didn't even bother to button her coat. "You didn't know the party would be outside, did you?"

"Nova didn't mention it," Harper says. "I should have probably asked. I'm a little overdressed for a slumber party, but I just came from—"

"A hot date?" I guess, hoping that I'm dead wrong.

Harper shakes her head no and smiles. "A job interview for an internship for next semester."

And she wore *that* ensemble? It's sexy, breathtaking, and makes her look hot, and sure, it could be seen as professional. It's not exactly shimmery or revealing too much cleavage. It's just so red that it screams *hot and sexy* to me, but everything she wears looks good on her.

I've also never seen her in a dress before today, and the longer I stare at her, the more I feel like a bull ready to charge.

My cock certainly notices every curve on her luscious body.

"I brought a pair of pajamas for tonight to change into, but I forgot to pack another set of clothes unless I wear tomorrow's outfit now…" her voice trails off as she realizes her mistake.

"You can borrow something of mine," I offer.

Harper's eyes lighten up, relieved. "Are you sure?"

"It's fine. I have a duffel bag around back. Take whatever you need." I didn't exactly bring extra clothes, but I'll make do with what I have.

"Thanks."

"Come on, I'll take you inside and show you where you can get changed," I say. While I don't want to step foot inside the compound, I knew it was inevitable. And I'd rather keep an eye on Harper, protect her, than let anything happen to her. Not that I'd suspect my father of ever laying a finger on her.

He's not that type of monster.

He orders hits and has other men do the killing.

I grab my bag from the back porch and lead Harper inside. "Is Nova here yet?" Harper asks, still holding on to the birthday present.

"Not yet," I say and shake my head. "Haven't seen her, but I'm sure she'll be here soon."

"I am a little early. The interview ended before I thought it would, and then I caught the earlier train, and honestly, I was just hoping I could sit down and relax for a few minutes before all her friends show up. Sometimes I get nervous around new people."

I never knew Harper had anxiety. Is that why she doesn't come to the parties that we throw?

"Well, I'm here," I offer and lead her inside. "I'm not new." I hold the door for her, and once she's inside, I close it and lead her down the hallway, past the first door on the left and to the second door, which is the guest bathroom.

I offer her my entire wardrobe, my duffel bag, and bring it into the bathroom, placing it on the long bathroom sink counter for her. "Take whatever you need. Make sure you dress warm since we'll be outside for a bit. Ashton and I are going to get a bonfire started soon for you girls."

"Oh, that sounds perfect," Harper says with a smile as she unzips my bag and retrieves the box of condoms lying on top. "Were you planning on something?" she asks pointedly, tilting her head as she stares up at me.

"Better to be safe than sorry." I laugh and back out of the bathroom, leaving her to search through my bag while I wait in the hallway for her to finish changing.

I lean against the wall, mentally chastising myself for bringing the entire box of condoms from home. One or two would have sufficed, since it's not as though anything has happened between Harper and me.

Yes, I've wanted it to happen. Every time I stare into her eyes, smell her sweet scent, or brush up against her, I have wanton thoughts of her naked and writhing between the sheets. I've been playing it slow because I know that's what she needs, but it's agonizing and tearing me up inside, the desire building like a volcano ready to erupt.

And I swear she feels it too.

"Luca," Moreno says as he walks by, carrying a set of papers with him. "It's good to see you home for Nova's birthday party."

"I wouldn't miss it for the world," I say, putting on a forced smile. While I love Nova, if it hadn't been for Harper showing up, I wouldn't be here.

Last year, Nova and I celebrated her birthday at the lake. I bought her a new set of ice skates and we went skating. It was a nice gift and an easy way to stay out of the compound. This year, I wasn't as lucky.

"Dante will be pleased to see you," Moreno says, and his eyes crinkle just a bit, as though he's realizing that he may not even believe his own words.

"You and I both know that isn't quite fact."

"He does care for you, in his own way," he says.

He has to defend Dante. After all, he works for him, is second in command, and would do anything to protect the don.

"We both know I grew up to be a disappointment to him." I don't pretend otherwise. It would be foolish to think Dante loves me. He loves my mother, although I'll never know how a man so cold as him can love anyone. I fold my arms across my chest, leaning back against the wall.

The bathroom door opens, and Moreno glances at the open door to reveal Harper. She's wearing my Evergreen University sweatshirt, which is big on her but looks absolutely sinful, and my sweatpants that I planned to wear around here for bed. Usually, I sleep in boxers or in the buff, which might end up happening after all.

"And who is this young lady?" Moreno asks, raising a curious eye at the strange blonde and then at me.

"I'm Harper," she says, holding out her hand to introduce herself.

"She's my girlfriend," I say, stepping closer to Harper protectively. While I don't think Moreno would cause any harm to come to her, I also don't want to take any chances. I also know that Nova's parents aren't aware that she's been spending a bit of time at the university with us, and I'm trying to keep her out of further trouble.

Harper catches my stare and gives me a quizzical look. "Yes," she says and doesn't further elaborate. She hands me back my bag of clothes. "Thanks," she says, staring at me, and leans in, pressing a soft kiss to my cheek.

If she's playing the doting fake girlfriend, then I could definitely get on board with this scenario.

The backdoor swings open, and Mom comes waltzing inside with Nova behind her.

"Nova!" Moreno says, pleased to see his daughter. "You're home late. You've already got guests attending your party."

"We're hardly guests," I say, "just me and my girlfriend." I grab Harper's hand before she can think twice about this situation and intertwine our fingers together.

Nova tilts her head slightly, a look of confusion on her face, and I'm not sure if she's well aware of the game we're playing for her benefit.

"Honey, you didn't tell me you were dating anyone," Mom says, her eyes wide with excitement as she hurries across the hallway and toward Harper.

I want to apologize to Harper, but the words don't come, and instead, Mom grabs Harper and pulls her into a hug, yanking our hands free. The duffel bag between us falls to the floor in a heap, which is pretty much how I feel, a bit out of sorts. And this is entirely my doing.

Nova stalks over to me, giving me a look that says *what the fuck are you up to? Is this for real?*

I hurry over to Nova, embracing her in a hug. "Long time, no see," I say and whisper into her ear, "I'm trying to protect you since they don't know you've been visiting us."

"Thanks," Nova whispers.

"We brought you a present," I say and nod toward the gift that Harper is holding.

Harper shoots daggers at me as she hands the gift bag over to Nova. "You did not help in the least bit with this gift," my fake girlfriend sells me out. "I asked you what I should get her, and you blew me off."

"Sounds just like my son," Mom says. "Come on into the kitchen. Let's grab some hot cocoa."

"Mom, Ashton is outside, and we should get the bonfire started soon."

"Bonfire?" Nova asks, glancing at me, confused.

"Yeah, I know you wanted a sleepover, you kept texting me how you wanted to do a girls' night, and I thought it'd be great to make a huge bonfire and maybe do a sleeping under the stars party for your birthday."

"It's a bit cold outside for that," Mom points out, and I know she's right.

"I could run out to the store and buy a couple of tents for the kids," Moreno offers.

"We're not kids," Nova huffs. "We'll enjoy the bonfire and then we can crash in my room. There's plenty of space for the party. Ember and Violetta already canceled. Right now, it's just the three of us."

"Four," I say.

Nova gives me a confused look.

"Ashton is outside," I say.

Nova nods. "Oh, right."

Moreno rubs at his jaw. "If your friends aren't spending the night, then I'm sure these guys don't want to all crash in your bedroom. We'll make sure the guest rooms are ready for this evening."

"That isn't necessary," I say.

"Where do you plan on sleeping?" Mom asks.

"After the bonfire, we were planning on driving back to university and spending the night at home," I say.

"Nonsense," Mom says. "This is your home."

Moreno clears his throat. "Then why did you and Ashton both bring duffel bags with you?" His stare alone reminds me that he's interrogated men for a living.

"We'd love to stay over," Harper says, cutting the tension with a smile. She wraps her arm around my waist, pulling me against her. "Wouldn't we, babe?" Leaning up on her tiptoes, she plants another soft, chaste kiss on my cheek.

She has no idea what's happening, the intensity of which I'm dying inside every minute under this roof reminds me of the hell I've witnessed and the bloodshed I've seen. I tried to bury it, move on, and forget the things I saw as a child in the basement.

Harper has no idea about any of it, because I've never told her.

Why would I?

We're not dating. We're friends, and that kind of secret isn't safe with a friend. It's the kind of secret that gets someone killed.

Mom watches us, a warm smile on her face. I'm not sure, but it seems like she's buying the girlfriend act.

Moreno, though, he seems a bit more suspicious, probably because that's his job. He's suspicious of everyone.

———————

Seated around the campfire outside on lawn chairs, Harper is next to me. She's leaning forward in her chair, roasting a marshmallow for s'mores. I want to pull her into my lap, have her sit with me, but it's only the four of us outside, and I doubt she'd be comfortable playing *fake girlfriend* outside.

"I'm sorry your other friends didn't make it," Harper says. "But I'm here, and I'm willing to do whatever crazy slumber party stuff you still want to do. Hair. Nails—"

"Pillow fight," Ashton quips with a grin.

"I'll throw a pillow at your face," Nova says and sticks her tongue out at him. "Boys are always such pervs!"

"Not all boys," I say. "Just the ones on the hockey team, so stay away from all of them."

Nova rolls her eyes. "I know. You've made it clear not to date anyone on your team, your roommates, anyone you know. Well, guess what? Next semester, I'll be at Evergreen with you."

I groan—just thinking about her trying to hook up with someone makes my skin crawl. "Do me a favor and save yourself until marriage."

Harper laughs. "Right, because that's what you've done. You guys are all the same, such hypocrites."

Frowning, I shift in my seat, turning to face Harper. "Why do you think that?"

"Oh, like you haven't slept your way through the girls at EU?" She's staring at me, waiting for me to challenge her, and the thing is she's right.

I've slept with plenty of girls, none of them recently, since I've had my eye on Harper, but freshman year, I certainly had a lot of fun.

"Not all of them," I counter, staring at her. "I know one I'd like to fuck."

She glares at me and unceremoniously dunks her marshmallow in the fire. "Aww, shit," she curses as it falls into the flames. She shoots the empty poker out of the fire, directing it at me.

"Distracted?" I laugh but lean back, careful not to get stabbed by the hot poker.

"So, are you two actually dating, or what?" Nova asks, grabbing another marshmallow from the bag. She helps put it on the stick for Harper, which I'd have been happy to do if she wasn't pointing that hot rod of fire at me.

"Thanks," Harper says, roasting her second marshmallow for the night.

Good thing there's an entire fresh bag of jumbo marshmallows, because I have a feeling we'll be going through quite a few of them this evening.

Nova grabs a marshmallow for herself and shoves the entire unroasted treat into her mouth. The girl has zero patience.

"You don't roast them first?" Ashton asks, raising an eyebrow at Nova.

Nova shrugs. "I could, but it takes too long."

Ashton shakes his head, stands, and grabs another roasting stick. He slides three marshmallows onto the stick before bringing it to rest just above the fire. "How toasted do you like them?"

"Not burned," Nova says. "Don't do a Harper and light that sucker on fire."

"I got distracted," Harper says defensively.

"Which brings us back to the question, are you two dating?" Nova asks, glancing between Harper and me.

"Can't really be dating a guy if he's taking your roommate home and kissing her outside your dorm room," Harper says.

My jaw tenses. Shit. She's still pissed about that? I thought we were over what happened the other night.

Ashton's eyes widen. "You didn't tell me you kissed Quinn."

"Quinn, okay," Nova says, repeating her name, "and you knew about her?" She's staring at Ashton, confused.

"I was in the car waiting for his ass to take me home."

"I'll bet you won't ask for a ride from me again after a game," I say. It isn't intended to be harsh, but it certainly comes out that way. I'm pissed that Harper brought up Quinn, and even more upset that Ashton had to continue the conversation instead of being a friend and helping defend what happened. He was there after the game. He saw her outside in the cold. Was I supposed to leave her to freeze to death?

"Please don't fight on my birthday," Nova says, staring at me, giving me that look that could break hearts.

"I'm not fighting," I say.

"Could have fooled me," Ashton quips. "So, you two aren't dating?" He looks from Harper to me, and I swear there's a glint in his eye, like he's feeling hopeful.

I stand, ready to defend the fact that Harper is *mine*. Even if we're not dating, there's zero chance of Ashton getting his hands on her.

"Sit down," Harper snarls at me, and I swear I can see steam emanating from her.

Or maybe it's the fire that's wafting in her direction. Could be a bit of both, actually.

"We're taking things at a glacial pace," Harper says,

her tone much calmer than her snap at me seconds earlier.

"That's putting it mildly," I say. Although she's right, glacial does seem to be explaining our dating style, if you can even call in that. We've kissed, and it was everything I could have imagined, but so much better. And I crave more. I know she does too, so what's holding her back?

"Maybe if you didn't kiss Quinn, it wouldn't be so glacial," Nova says pointedly.

I can't believe Nova is defending Harper instead of me. She ought to know that I haven't been bringing Quinn or anyone else around this semester. She's over often enough to see that the only girl I'm hanging around is Harper.

"I'm just protecting my heart," Harper whispers, but I hear her, and I'm pretty sure everyone around the campfire catches her whisper along with the wind.

"Luca won't hurt you," Nova says, her voice just as soft, "and if he does, I'll kill him myself for you."

My little sister glares at me.

"Point taken," I say and exhale a heavy sigh.

"Hey, boyfriend," Harper teases, handing me the hot poker hovering over the fire with the marshmallow slowly roasting. "Your mom mentioned hot cocoa. Do you think I could go inside and make some?" She stands, stretching her legs while I take the metal stick she's been holding from her and continue roasting her marshmallow.

I really don't want her to go inside the house alone.

"Can it wait until this is done?" I ask, nodding toward the marshmallow. "It'll just be another minute. Then I'll go inside with you, and we can make hot chocolate together."

"How romantic," Nova teases, "but she's my friend and I'll make hot chocolate with her." She stands and gestures for Harper to follow her into the house.

"I'm going to eat your marshmallow if it gets done," I threaten playfully.

Harper shrugs. "There's more. I saw the huge bag. I'm not worried." She follows Nova inside, and I momentarily hold my breath, watching them enter the compound.

"You okay?" Ashton asks. It's just the two of us outside, although we're never really alone. There are cameras around the entire house, inside and out.

"Fine," I say, lying to Ashton. I can't explain it to him; he wouldn't understand. Yes, his father is mafia, but he's talked about following in his footsteps when he finishes school, working for the family business. It's why he's in college, majoring in Criminology, with a minor in Forensic Accounting. It all sounds boring as fuck to me.

Less than two minutes later, I hear the girls chatter, and I glance over my shoulder as they approach. "That was weird," Nova says.

"Is he usually like that?" Harper asks, his brow pinched as they stalk back to the fire. Harper sits back down beside me, holding out her hand for the hot poker, which now has a perfectly roasted marshmallow waiting for her.

Except I decide to be a bit of an ass and pull the marshmallow off, bringing it to my lips.

"Hey! That's mine!" Her eyes widen in horror.

"I told you if you left it with me, I was going to eat it." I shove the sticky treat in my mouth before she can snatch it from me.

Harper's eyes narrow, and she climbs onto my chair, straddling me.

Surprised by her movements, my hand fumbles with the hot poker, letting it fall to the ground. It's not like I need it anymore anyhow. The hand that held the marshmallow gets yanked away from my lips as she tries to grab for the fluffy treat, but it's too late. It's already in my mouth.

"That's *my* marshmallow," Harper seethes, her tongue darting out, tasting the gooeyness at the corner of my lips before closing the distance.

My mouth is completely full of hot, sticky marshmallow, and she's clawing at me like a beast ready for her kill.

Damn, if I knew she had a thing for roasted marshmallows, I'd have teased her with them sooner.

Her mouth caresses mine, her tongue forcing my lips apart as she tries to steal a taste. The kiss isn't soft and sweet. It's rough and fueled with determination. She wants what's mine.

I grip her hips with my hands, pulling her closer and

tighter against me. Does she have any idea what she does to me?

"No one comes inside until Moreno or me tells you it's time. Is that clear?" Dante's voice echoes from behind me.

Harper immediately pulls back, but she stays on my lap, my hands trapping her against me.

When the hell did he come outside?

"We know," Nova says with an exasperated sigh. "You already chased us out when we were making hot chocolate." There's a bit of a snippy tone in her demeanor, and I can't say I blame her.

I'm always snippy with Dante.

There's only one reason Dante would keep us out of the house, and that's because trouble is brewing inside.

"I came out here to make sure the message was clear for everyone," he says.

"Understood, sir," Ashton says.

"Son?"

It pains me to hear him call me *that*. I wince. "Yeah, I heard you, Dante."

He hates when I call him that. Dante is my biological father. It's not as though he's my stepfather, and there's been more times than I can count that he's scolded me or shouted at me for not giving him the respect that he deserves. I wait to embrace another tongue-lashing. He's never physically abused me. He doesn't have to for me to know that he's a monster.

Dante shakes his head. "I don't have time for your antics," he mutters, heading back inside the compound. The sliding glass door slams with a resounding thud, and I can practically hear the curtains being shut from inside, keeping all prying eyes out.

Harper pulls back, but I keep my hands on her hips, holding her in place. She raises an eyebrow at me. "The girlfriend show is over; your father is back inside the house. Which, I might add, you forgot to mention he's weird."

"Why do you think I avoid him like the plague?" I grumble.

"Yeah, that's why," Ashton says and rolls his eyes. I shoot him a look to shut up. I don't need to worry Harper or have her any more involved than she already is. The fact Dante came outside to tell us to keep the fuck out of the house tells me all I need to know.

They're bringing in someone for interrogation.

My stomach roils just thinking about the poor soul who betrayed the Ricci family. Hopefully, they're not a father or married. If they're lucky, maybe no one will notice or care that they've gone missing.

It's unlikely they'll return home.

Moreno and Dante don't take prisoners for entertainment. They interrogate because they require information, and when that information is obtained, those men are of no use to them.

"I can't believe we got kicked out of the house during my own birthday party," Nova says, groaning under her breath.

"Maybe they're making you a birthday cake and don't want to ruin the surprise by you seeing it before it's ready?" Harper quips.

I brush a strand of hair behind her ear, my thumb stroking her cheek. "That's sweet," I whisper, *but completely foolish.*

Harper smiles and shrugs. "I'm glad you gave me your sweatshirt. It's freezing out here!"

"I know a few ways to get you to warm up," I say suggestively.

She smacks my arm and climbs off my chair, grabbing the stick to add another marshmallow to roast. Harper sits back down in her own chair, bringing it slightly closer to the fire to keep warm.

I stand, grabbing a few more logs, tossing them carefully into the fire to keep it roaring. It is chilly outside. Thankfully, I was already dressed warmly before arriving at the compound.

Ashton clears his throat, glancing between Harper and me. "So that little marshmallow debacle back there, was that entirely a performance for his father?" he asks.

It's certainly a question roiling through my mind at the moment. I give props to Ashton for bringing it up.

"You did say I was your girlfriend," Harper smiles at me. "I was just playing the role."

Nova snorts with laughter. "Sure, keep telling yourself that, Harper."

Harper's eyes narrow. "I thought you were on my side, *friend*."

My little sister tosses her arms up in the air. "Truce. Don't make me pick a side. It's *my* birthday, remember?"

"Fine." Harper laughs. "Are you going to open your birthday present?" She gestures to the gift bag sitting at Nova's feet.

"Oh, sure! We usually do that after cake, but who knows when we'll have dessert." Nova grabs the gift bag and places it onto her lap. She grabs the card first, opening it. It's grown dark outside, and she grabs her phone and turns the flashlight feature on, allowing her to read the card. "Cute."

"Are you going to share with the group?" Ashton asks, waiting for her to hand over the card for everyone to read.

Nova laughs. "No! When it's your birthday, you can read your own card." Her hands dig into the bag, pulling out an adorable narwhal stuffed animal, and I can't help but wonder if she chose that because it's my team's mascot.

My heart fills with pride.

"Oh my gosh! Isn't he adorable?" Nova squeals and brings it to her face and nuzzles its horn. "I can't wait until I start there next semester!"

"There's a gift card in there too," Harper says, gesturing to the bag.

Nova's eyes light up even more and she feels around, finding it and looking at it with the flashlight. "Oh, bookstore! Yes! We are going first thing tomorrow morning so I can grab a new book."

Her excitement is contagious.

"Okay," Harper says and smiles. "Sounds fun."

"What'd you get me?" Nova asks, turning to face me.

"He probably brought you dirty laundry," Ashton jokes, and he stands. "My gift is in my bag. Give me a second to grab it." He heads over toward the house, but his bags are still outside on the porch. He digs through, and a minute later, he returns with a wrapped box.

Shit.

I rub the back of my neck awkwardly.

I didn't have time to get Nova a present, and not because I didn't want to, but between school and hockey practice, I haven't exactly gone off campus. If I'd thought ahead, I could have ordered her a present ... but she hasn't been the first thought on my mind lately.

I'll think of something before the night is over. I can always have Moreno swing by the store and pick it up if I give him cash. Wouldn't be the first time he's made a run for a last-minute gift.

Nova's eyes light up as Ashton carries over a box that was small enough to fit into his backpack but isn't so tiny that it could be jewelry.

Thank heaven.

I'd have had a fit if he'd bought her a piece of jewelry.

That's way too intimate a gift to be giving to Nova.

Ashton hands the gift-wrapped present to Nova. "Happy Birthday," he says and smiles at her.

Her eyes crinkle as she takes the present and holds it up to her ear, gently shaking it. "It's not a puppy."

Ashton laughs and throws his head back. "Definitely not a pet."

"Are you going to open it, or keep us all in suspense?" I ask.

Nova glances at me peculiarly and then shakes her head, dismissing whatever thought that traverses through her head. She doesn't say anything, just rips the birthday wrapping paper off the box and reveals a brown box.

She raises an inquisitive eyebrow and opens the box, pulling out an eyeshadow palette and perfume. "Oh my gosh. It's gorgeous!" She squeals with delight and then opens the perfume from its box, unwrapping the contents to smell the bottle. "Thank you, Ashton!" Her excitement is overflowing with glee.

"You bought her makeup," I say, unsure what to make of the gift he gave her.

"I love it!" Nova says excitedly.

"I didn't know you wear makeup." I stare at her, surprised.

"There's a lot you don't know," Nova says and shrugs. "You're always with your *fake girlfriend*."

"We're always studying together," Harper says. She carefully pulls the marshmallow from the stick and takes a bite, her eyes closing in perfect bliss.

She looks sexy as hell.

It takes everything in my power not to waltz over and capture her mouth with mine, kissing her, tasting her, devouring that marshmallow along with her.

Fuck.

When did I fall so damn hard for Harper McKenna?

"You're staring," Harper mumbles, the marshmallow in her mouth as she catches my gaze on her.

NINE

HARPER

"When do I get to open my present from you?" Nova asks, her gaze fierce as she waits for Luca to hand over his present.

I get the distinct impression that he didn't bring her a gift, which seems quite unlike Luca. Maybe he left it at home and is embarrassed not to have it with him?

"Later," he says with a smirk.

Nova groans and rolls her eyes. A typical teenager move. "Whatever. You weren't even invited to my birthday party. It was supposed to be girls only. Remember."

"I think it's nice that Luca and Ashton decided to join us," I quip, trying to ease the mounting tension. I don't point out that her friends bailed last minute, and otherwise, it would have been just the two of us if the boys hadn't decided to drive up and stay over for the night.

Plus, the bonfire was a nice suggestion.

I stretch from the lawn chair, needing to move around. My legs are getting achy, and my butt is sore and a tad numb from sitting for so long. It might also be the cold getting to me. I'm not a fan of winter.

I keep my hands buried in the sweatshirt I'm wearing. It smells distinctly of Luca, and I try not to take a huge whiff, or he'll probably notice and chide me for being weird.

It smells like him, though, and I hate to admit I like it, a lot.

"Are you okay?" Luca asks, glancing up at me as I tower above him, shuffling my feet.

He's sitting in the lawn chair, enjoying the warmth of the fire.

"Yeah, I just, I need to use the bathroom. Do you think they'll care if I wander inside? I mean, if they're planning a surprise for Nova, she's the one they want to keep out of the house."

Luca clears his throat, his eyes widen, and he stands. "You can't just go barging into the house."

I don't know what the big deal is. It's not like we weren't inside earlier. "I have to pee. I'm either going to do it out here or inside."

Ashton and Luca exchange a glance.

"What?" I ask, looking between them. What aren't they saying?

"Fine, I'll walk you inside," Luca says and takes my arm, guiding me toward the house.

"I can find the bathroom myself," I say, unsure why the theatrics. Luca accompanies me to the back porch as we approach the door.

"Yeah, well, they asked us not to come inside until they were ready for us," he reminds me. He knocks on the glass door and then goes to slowly open it when a man appears on the other side of the closed curtain.

I don't recognize the gentleman, but he's tall, a bit stocky, and bald. He's got black slacks, and as he opens the door farther, I realize he's wearing a suit.

Luca leans in, whispers something to the gentleman, and he glances at me.

The man isn't quite dressed as a butler, but I can't put my finger on why this man is standing at the back door, dressed in a black business suit, looking more like a bodyguard than anything else.

"I have to pee," I say, interrupting whatever exchange is happening quietly between Luca and the mysterious man at the back door. "Can you let me in, or do you want me to go pee in the lawn like an animal?"

I'm joking, but the man doesn't laugh, and Luca, I swear, forces a smile.

"She's kidding. But she does need to use the bathroom."

The bodyguard clears his throat, glances over his shoulder and grumbles. "Make it quick. Your father will have my head if he sees you inside."

The mysterious man opens the back door farther, granting us entrance inside.

Luca grabs my arm and hurries me down the hallway. He's practically running for the bathroom.

"Slow down," I chide. "I'm not actually going to pee myself." I do have to go, but the fact is I can walk to the bathroom like a normal person. I don't need to run like a toddler who is potty-training.

Luca doesn't say anything, just ushers me to the bathroom on the left, pushes open the door, flips on the light and fan and practically shoves me inside. "Be quick," he recants.

"Fine. I'll pee quickly, just for you."

I shut the bathroom door and do my business, relieved when I finally get to sit on a toilet. And it's a warm toilet. The unit actually has a heated feature.

"Swanky," I mumble, finishing up and washing my hands. I glance at my reflection in the mirror.

My cheeks are rosy from the cold, and so is my nose. "I look like Rudolph," I mutter, shutting off the sink and drying my hands.

I unlock the bathroom door and pull it open. "Do you want to go? It's nice in there, heated toilet seat and all." I point behind myself.

Luca abruptly shakes his head. "Let's go back outside." He saddles up next to me, his hand on my lower back as he begins ushering me down the hallway, back the way we came in hastily.

"Can we grab some hot chocolate, please?" I ask and pause near the entrance to the kitchen. The window overlooks the backyard, but the blinds are closed, and I can't see the bonfire from inside. "It's getting chilly outside. My fingers could really use a warm mug to help keep them toasty."

"Of course," he says and presses a kiss to my cheek. The warm gesture sends tingles throughout my body. I glance around, and there's only the mysterious bodyguard standing near the door. His parents are nowhere in sight.

"What was that for?" I ask, staring up at him.

"Do I have to have a reason to kiss you?" Luca asks. He smiles at me, and my stomach flutters with a thousand butterflies all at once. "I'll get the hot water started on the kettle, and you can go keep Nova company outside. I'm sure she's dying of boredom with Ashton outside alone."

He leads me to the back door, and the bodyguard opens the back door, letting me back outside.

"Weird," I mumble to myself. I head for the bonfire, nearly tripping over my own feet, but thankfully I manage to catch myself before face-planting onto the grass.

That would have been embarrassing.

"Where's Luca?" Ashton asks, glancing at me.

"He's putting on the kettle to make some hot cocoa." I sit back down on my lawn chair beside Nova. She hands me the bag of marshmallows.

"Hot chocolate must have marshmallows. The hot chocolate in the house is missing the best ingredient," Nova says.

———

After Nova gets tired of the bonfire and we're invited back into the house for cake, Luca produces a present wrapped haphazardly in birthday paper. Although it looks like two rolls of different gift-wrap.

It's a huge box, and I'm not quite sure when he brought it inside. He must have done so when we clearly weren't looking.

"Sorry, I ran out of wrapping paper. The dollar store stuff wasn't a full roll."

Nova laughs and shrugs. "Do you think I care about the wrapping paper? It's huge! What is it?"

"Open it," Luca says and leans back against the kitchen wall.

I could have sworn he didn't get her anything, but maybe he was hiding his present all along?

Both of her parents are in the kitchen. Paige is nursing a glass of wine, and Moreno keeps glancing at his phone, clearly distracted by something—I'm guessing his job. He's still in a suit. The man looks like he hasn't gotten off work yet, and it's well past ten o'clock.

I'm on my third cup of hot cocoa, craving chocolate, and it's absolutely delicious. I swear Luca put something in it that makes me want another cup.

Nova tears the wrapping paper off the cardboard box. She yanks open the box and pulls out packaging paper, looking inside for her present. The box is huge, knee high and the amount of paper just keeps coming out.

"Did you forget the present?" Nova asks.

Luca grins. "It's two presents in one. A moving box."

Nova's eyes narrow. "I don't get it."

Paige smiles, like she's in on the surprise, or maybe she has an inkling of an idea what Luca got her as a gift.

"Since you're attending EU next semester, you'll have a place to stay with us. Jessie graduates early, and when he moves out, you'll have a place this winter to move into, if you want to live with us."

Nova's eyes widen, and she takes a step back, clearly overwhelmed.

"Wait. You want me to move into your gross apartment? No way!" Her nose scrunches up in disgust. "You boys never clean that place. I'm not moving in to be your housemaid or whatever. Worst gift ever, Luca." She tosses her hand up and gives him the finger.

"Nova!" Paige scolds her daughter.

Moreno ignores the entire exchange, texting on his phone as he's physically present in the kitchen, but mentally, he's a million miles away.

Is that how Luca's parents are as well? He certainly seems closer to his mother than his father, at least the brief encounters I've seen at their house today.

"Keep digging. There's a gift card at the bottom," Luca says.

Nova rolls her eyes and lifts the entire box, tossing it upside down, allowing all the contents to drop to the kitchen floor and spill out. She fumbles around through the paper, finally finding a small envelope with a gift card inside.

She tears open the envelope and squeals. "Holy cow! It's two hundred dollars for a spa day!" she squeals with delight.

"I thought you might take your new bestie with you," Luca says, nodding toward me.

"That was really nice of you," I say, taking his hand and giving it a squeeze. Not that I was expecting to be included in the spa day present, but that he clearly spent quite a bit on her birthday. Not to mention inviting her to live with him. Although I don't blame her for being grossed out at the idea of living with her brother and his teammates.

I'm not entirely sure he really thought that through, unless he was hoping to keep an eye on her. He's made it clear to his teammates that she's off-limits. I've heard the way Luca talks; he's protective of Nova.

It's actually quite sweet.

"Happy eighteenth birthday, Nova," he says. "I'm really excited that you'll be joining us next semester at Evergreen."

She throws her arms around Luca, clearly pleased with his gift, at least the spa package.

Paige and Moreno smile and glance at each other. He's finally off his phone, at least for the moment. "We have a gift for you, too, sweetheart," Paige says.

"Why don't you come outside for a minute?" Moreno says, gesturing for everyone to follow him down the main corridor and to the front entrance.

The house is massive. It's three stories and clearly well-kept. It could easily house several families inside, which, apparently, it does, since Nova and Luca grew up together.

I find that a bit strange, especially since they're not related. At least that's what Luca had mentioned. But maybe Moreno and Paige are related to his parents and Nova is adopted? I try to wrap my head around their family tree and then finally give up. What's the point? Why does it even matter? If it works for them, so be it.

We head to the front door, and Nova yanks it open.

Moreno hands Nova a set of car keys to a two-door silver hatchback. "Happy Birthday."

"You guys got me a car!"

"Glad I didn't have to follow *that*," Luca whispers into my ear.

————

Nova is seated across from me on her bedroom floor, an array of nail polish with dozens of choices ranging from glitter to gel and everything in-between. I've finished painting my fingers and toes.

The boys are situated on her bed above us. I grab Luca's leg and wiggle down his sock.

"What are you doing, Harper?" He glares at me because he must already know what I'm planning on doing.

"Giving you a pedicure. Relax," I say and grin at Nova. "Which do you think is his color?" I wrangle two bottles in one hand, blue and purple, showing it to Nova.

"Definitely purple," she says with a giggle.

"Hell no!" Luca growls at me, and my fingers fumble with the nail polish. Thankfully, both bottles are closed tight.

My fingers stay firmly wrapped around his ankle. "So, blue it is."

"Just let them do it," Ashton says, gesturing at the two of us on the floor. "It's not like anyone looks at your feet."

"I look at my feet!" Luca says, as if that's explanation enough to stop us.

Nova finishes the last of her toes and points at Ashton. "What color will it be?"

He exhales softly, and his gaze peruses the colors

laid out on the floor. "Color my toes the same as the Narwhals." He beams proudly.

"Teal and white. Got it." Nova grabs the two colors. "I'll paint your toes teal and then add some white highlights."

"You do realize no one is ever going to see this?" Luca says, staring pointedly at Nova.

"I know, that's why you're getting a manicure next," I say.

Luca blows out a puff of steam. "Fine, but you'd better be able to spell out Narwhals on my fingernails."

Nova's eyes light up. "Oh, I can definitely do that!"

Ashton's smiling and points at me. "No, Harper has to do his nails. You're doing mine. Fingers and toes, baby." He wiggles his fingers at Nova, giving in to her delight.

"You're not going to fight me?" Nova stares up at him, surprised.

Ashton shrugs. "No reason; I'm secure in my masculinity," he touts, smirking at Luca.

"Jackass." Luca throws up his middle finger at Ashton.

An hour later, after the nail polish is put away and Nova is yawning but fighting sleep, we're shown to the guest rooms for the night.

Luca leads me to the guest room. "I'll be right next door if you need anything," he says, pointing at his room.

"Is that your childhood bedroom?" I ask, pausing in the hallway, wanting to catch a glimpse inside.

"It is, but there really isn't anything of mine in there anymore," he says.

"What do you mean?"

"I'll show you," he says and leads me into his bedroom. It feels cold, although the temperature is ambient. The walls are bare and painted a crème that makes the room feel even more bland.

There aren't any pictures on the dresser in the far corner of the room. The nightstand houses a digital clock. The room looks like someone forgot to decorate it.

"This was your bedroom?" I ask. There's no sign of Luca, except for his duffel bag seated on the mattress. No evidence that he's ever played hockey. No trophies or ribbons. No posters. Nothing that screams this was ever a teenage boy's room.

"Like I said, there's not anything of mine in here anymore."

It's sad, and my heart breaks as I reach for his hand. It's almost like they had him erased.

Meanwhile, my bedroom at home still has the framed prints autographed by one of my favorite authors. I have a jewelry rack hanging on my wall beside the door with my necklaces, and my dresser has my rings and earrings safely secured and waiting for me when I come home to visit. There are posters hanging on my walls, featuring my favorite music artists and even a signed movie poster from when I went to the local comic book convention last summer.

There's absolutely no trace of Luca in his childhood bedroom, and honestly, it makes me sad.

"Did you take everything with you when you moved out?" I ask. I'm trying to make sense of the situation.

He lives in an apartment; I'm in the dorms. He has a lot more space, his own bedroom, while I'm forced to share my space with Quinn.

"Hardly. Mom saved a couple of boxes of my stuff and had it put into the attic."

I wave my hand at the bare room. "Was this Dante's idea?" I ask, assuming his father is to blame. Tonight, I've heard the way he speaks about him, *to him*, and it's obvious they don't get along. I'm just not sure why.

He laughs under his breath. It's a dark laugh, filled with anger and pain. "You could say that."

"What do you mean?"

"He wanted me erased."

"Did something happen between you and him or..." my words trail off. Perhaps he never wanted a child at all.

He glances away, unwilling to meet my stare. "That's a story for never," Luca says. He exhales a breath after a beat and finally turns toward me. "Let's get you ready for bed, in your room. Unless you want to sleep with me?"

My breath catches in my throat.

I reach for his hand, intertwining our fingers together, pulling him closer to me.

There's a sadness, a coldness enveloped around him, and I want to ease it all away.

He's clearly hurting, and I don't want him to be in pain.

"Can I sleep in here with you?" I ask, my voice soft, tentative. I'm almost afraid his offer was a joke, and he's going to tell me to go back into my room tonight for bed.

Luca leans in, pressing his forehead against mine. The heat of his breath, his touch, the feel of his energy surrounding me is enough to make me warm and tingly.

He untangles our hands, only so that he can touch my face. Cupping my cheek, he stares into my eyes, waiting to kiss me.

What is he waiting for?

"I think I can make room for you in my bed," Luca says with a wry smile and pulls me closer against him.

I can feel the rise and fall of his chest as he's pressed tight. The backs of his fingers graze my cheek, staring at me as though he's memorizing every detail.

"Are you going to kiss me or just stare?" I grin, smiling up at him cheekily.

"I could watch you every morning and every evening, as easily as the sun rising and setting."

I nudge him with my shoulder. "Does that line work on all the girls?" I ask.

Luca smiles and shrugs. "Don't know, I've never tried it on anyone else." One hand remains on my cheek, his touch like a sizzle of electricity, the hum vibrating through me as he caresses my skin. His other hand slides down to my hip, the pads of his fingers soft and firm as he grazes my hip with his touch. "Believe it or not, Harper, I'm not the player you think I am."

His gaze stares into me, and I feel the air stolen from my lungs.

I don't know what to say.

"I haven't so much as thought about anyone since I met you," he whispers and presses a soft, chaste kiss to the corner of my lips.

I lean forward, my breath heavy, my lips parting, wanting to kiss him.

But he seems to have other ideas.

"That can't be true," I whisper, trying to think back to the girls who come up to him in class and in the hallway. Has he flirted with any of them back?

"I swear it is; even Ashton knows I've been celibate this year. I haven't brought another girl into my room."

A smile crosses my face. "Except for Nova," I say, reminding him of that time they threw a house party and I caught the two of them coming downstairs together.

"She doesn't count. She's a sister to me, you know that," Luca says and stares at me, making sure I realize that he's been honest with me, and perhaps even vulnerable.

"I see it now," I say and scrunch my nose up at him. "No more talking about your sister tonight."

"Fine with me." He closes the distance, his breath mingling with mine as he takes his time, kissing me softly and slowly on my nose, my cheek, and then my chin.

"Oh my gosh, will you just kiss me already?" I grumble and lean up on my tiptoes to crash my mouth onto his.

The man knows how to tease a girl. He probably gets off on it, making me squirm, all anxious and waiting for him.

He chuckles softly and pulls back, enough to stare into my gaze as both hands wrap around my hips. "I'm going to have to teach you some patience," he chides proudly, before letting his lips hover just above mine.

His fingers dance softly and aimlessly over my hips, inching the sweatshirt of his up just slightly so his touch is over bare skin.

I lean into him, craving more as he teases me endlessly, and it seems we're only getting started.

"I don't need patience," I mutter and lean in for the kill, or rather, kiss, in this case.

He pulls his back slightly out of reach, a smug look on his face. His hands still tease my hips, keeping my lower half firm against him, his touch tantalizing as his fingers skim the waistband of the sweatpants that I'm wearing.

"But I think you do," Luca says with conviction. There's a twinkle in his gray eyes. But behind those eyes, there's something darker lingering, heavier, fueled with want and need. "Your body is begging for me, but until your lips do the same, you're not ready for me."

My mouth drops, shocked.

And it's that surprise that lands his mouth on mine with a searing kiss, his tongue pushing past my lips, and I pull him closer, tighter, deeper.

Already, I crave more, but he seems to have other intentions as he breaks apart the kiss.

I'm gasping for breath, the room sweltering, and while his cheeks have a faint rosy hue, he seems otherwise calm, like he's just getting started on his brand of sweet torture.

"Did I leave you speechless?" He's teasing me, and

the man could easily kill me and I'd gladly fall into my own grave for him.

"I'm not going to beg for anything, ever," I say, my eyes narrowing.

As hot as Luca is, he will never see me beg.

Ever.

I walk him backward toward the mattress and gently push him down onto the bed. Straddling his hips, I climb above him, my hands on his chest.

"Are you sure about that?" he asks, smiling up at me. His hands tease my skin as I grind against him, and I watch as he's slowly becoming overloaded with pleasure.

We have too many clothes on, and I can certainly feel his excitement poking me.

About fucking time.

But he doesn't give in to temptation or pleasure. He's staring up at me, his back against the plush material as his fingers tease the hem of my shirt, inching the Evergreen University sweatshirt just slightly higher before his warm fingers guide upward as he brushes the pads of his fingers against the curve of my breast.

I inhale sharply and feel a pool of warmth flood through me.

His touch is pure electricity, humming and alive.

"You'll be the one begging," I say, staring down at him as my hips move against his.

His eyes momentarily close for a fraction of a second, and I watch all of his composure begin to melt away.

It's impossible not to feel powerful and pleased with the reaction I stir in him.

He shakes his head. "You'll beg," he whispers as I lean down and drag my tongue up his neck, tasting his skin before moving to his lips.

"I'm not so sure about that," I smirk and lean in, taking a taste, giving in to temptation as I let my body rest against him.

The kisses are hot and fierce, fueled with fire as he wraps his legs around my hips and rolls us over, pinning me on my back.

His body covers me for only a brief instant before he climbs off me, and I whimper.

"Don't worry," he says with a grin, "I'm not going anywhere. You're in *my bedroom*, remember?" Luca tugs off his shirt and guides me onto the mattress so that I can rest my head on the pillow while I watch him undress.

"Don't I get a strip show?" I joke and gesture for him to spin around while he's removing his clothes, so I get to enjoy the entire view.

"Next time," he promises, making it clear that this isn't a one-off fling happening.

He drops his sweats to the floor and stands naked in all his glory at the end of the bed.

I sit up and turn around, crawling on all fours on the mattress, wanting to taste and touch him. He's absolutely gorgeous, from his toned and tanned abs, all the way down his body.

Luca doesn't hide himself from me.

There's no reason to, and I love how comfortable he is naked. He's also got the body of an athlete, sculpted perfectly with thick muscles. He is truly a work of art.

It's hard not to stare.

He smiles and tilts his head with a crooked grin. "You ready to beg?" he asks.

I think he's joking, but I'm not entirely sure. I move onto my knees, wrapping my arms around his neck, pulling him against me, needing to feel him, to see that this is, in fact, real and I'm not dreaming.

"I think you're the one who's going to be begging," I whisper as I kiss him.

His body is warm beneath my touch, his muscles firm as my fingers trail across his stomach and down toward the juncture of his thighs.

He grabs my hand, guiding me onto my back, pushing my hands together into the mattress, trapping me.

It's exhilarating, and my body lights with fire as he holds me down against the bed. He's naked and warm, and I so want to feel skin on skin. This is torture. "Please," I whisper, and a knowing smile crosses his features.

"You listen so well," he says as he hovers over me.

It's sweltering, but I'm pretty sure the warmth is

entirely from the two of us. "I have too many clothes on."

"That's not begging." Luca smiles and releases his hold on me. "But you're right. You're overdressed, and I think it's time for your strip dance," he whispers into my ear.

My breath catches in my throat. The butterflies are back in my stomach. "I don't think I can do that," I whisper. "How about just strip?"

He smirks and climbs off me. "Be my guest." Luca offers me a hand, helping me off the mattress as I give him a confused look. "I would love to have you as my own personal stripper."

I choke on his words. "I didn't mean—" Humiliation creeping up on my face, I'm confident I'm blushing because it's hot as Hades in here.

Luca slowly helps me out of my clothes, the ones that he loaned me today for the bonfire. They tumble to the floor, and I can't help but feel inadequate, but those feelings are quickly silenced by his lips on my neck as he kisses a path down my body.

"Look at you," he whispers, moving down my breasts, "and you're *mine*." His voice comes out gravely and thick, heavy with desire. "You have no idea what you're doing to me."

He nips at my skin, kissing and tasting as my fingers tangle in his hair and move down across his back.

He lifts me to him, my legs wrapping around his waist as our lips meet once again, this time fueled with fire and flames. "God, I've wanted you for so long," he confesses between kisses.

Luca carries me to the mattress and guides me onto my back. He relinquishes his hold on me long enough to grab a condom from his overnight bag. "Aren't you glad I brought these?" He flashes the foil packet at me and drops it onto the mattress for later.

"I'm on the pill, Luca, but yes, I am glad that we're being safe. But again, do you really think you're going to need the entire box?"

"Gosh, I hope so." His lips are back against my skin, sending warm, tingly sensations throughout my body as he guides my thighs apart, but his lips move down my legs, teasing me. "I plan on memorizing every inch of you."

I try to keep my breathing and moans as quiet as possible. I grab a pillow, shoving it over my face as his mouth hovers between my legs. I don't know how thin the walls are and I don't want anyone hearing us, especially his family.

I can hear his soft chuckle, and he yanks the pillow away from my face. "Eyes on me, baby."

His commanding voice sends shivers through my core. I moan, and he smiles as his tongue teases along my folds, not quite touching me where I crave it the most. Luca knows exactly what he's doing. "That's my girl."

He's taking his sweet time, and his words send my body into overdrive, heat flooding all of my senses.

"Luca," I rasp, my fingers clenching at the bedsheets as I crave more. "I want to feel you inside of me." I'm not above begging at this point.

"You taste so fucking good." His mouth is on me, his tongue teasing my clit, driving me absolutely crazy.

His fingers hold my hips steady, his mouth never slowing down as he keeps the motions steady, the rhythm even, as I ride closer to oblivion.

"I want you to come for me," Luca commands, and my body willingly obeys him.

My toes curl and my eyes slam shut as I arch my back, feeling the beginning tremble ripple through me.

Gasping for air, my heart feels as though it will leap from my chest at any moment as my body shudders beneath him.

"Good girl," Luca says as he climbs back up my body, retrieving the foiled condom that's on the bed beside us.

My heart is still trying to catch up with my breathing. Lying on the mattress, my fingers stroke Luca, wanting to touch every inch of his body. "I want you inside of me," I say, making it clear that we're nowhere near done.

My insides tingle with warmth, and my body craves him. I've never had a man do that before—and succeed. Sure, my high school boyfriend would go down on me, but I never actually came from it.

I reach for Luca, my hands on his cheeks, pulling his mouth back down to me, needing to taste him. I crave him in the same way one needs air to breathe, but this is so much more intense. It's as though I'm drowning and he's the surface of the water that will keep me alive.

His mouth is back on mine, pushing his tongue inside, the condom secured as he teases my entrance with his cock, rubbing it against my clit.

I moan, gripping his shoulder with my fingernails. "Are you going to tease me all night?" I whisper, staring up at him.

"Just until you can't take it anymore," Luca says with a smile. "You have the perfect lips for kissing." And his mouth is back on mine, hungrily taking what he craves, *me*.

It's enough to make me feel as though my heart is going to burst within my chest. "Your—" I glance down between us. I don't know how he's going to fit inside.

He's fucking huge.

And I'm sure he's heard all the girls tell him that before, but it's true.

It makes me nervous as hell, because while I've had sex, it's been more than a year, and it was never anything like what Luca's sporting. His hard-on is big enough to scare a virgin.

Thank God I lost mine in high school to my shitty loser of a boyfriend.

"Have you ever—" Luca whispers. "If you haven't, we can take things slow." He's being so kind, and I know he doesn't want to slow things down, but I appreciate his willingness to meet my needs.

"I want you to fuck me, Luca," I say, giving him my enthusiastic consent, because while I'm scared that it's going to hurt, I also want this with him. And if any other girl were to get her claws on him, I might have to kill her.

The smile never leaves his face. "I've been waiting to hear you say that."

His fingers tease my pussy; one, and then two thick fingers stroke me, making sure I'm ready for him. He stretches me with a third finger, and as I moan, his lips cover mine. He's quick, withdrawing his fingers, and as I whimper from the loss of contact, he's slowly filling me with the tip of his cock.

I gasp, the pain so fucking exquisite that it's actually good, and he covers my lips again, this time nipping my bottom lip as I tremble beneath him.

"You can take it," he says, and his mouth is moving along my jawline to my ear. "You feel so fucking perfect."

I bend my knees, giving him ample access and then wrap my legs around him, pulling him deeper.

"Open your eyes and look what you're fucking doing to me," Luca rasps.

I struggle to keep my eyes open, to focus on *him*. Everything feels amazing, and my senses are on complete overload.

"You feel so fucking good," I whisper up at him, my nails gently scraping over his back and down to his ass, pulling him deeper and tighter.

He stretches me, but the pain dulls to a pleasant throbbing that intensifies in pure bliss as he slowly begins moving.

"Keep doing that," I gasp, feeling my body respond all over again, already.

Luca smirks, knowing full well the effect that he's having on me. His hips grind into mine, his thrusts slow and even until he begins picking up pace, and I've never been more grateful for a headboard as I claw at the wooden spindle, holding on as if my life depends on it.

My insides are on fire, feeling the second orgasm ready to rip through my existence as Luca's breathing comes out quicker, in pants.

"Fuck, I'm close. Again," I moan, wanting him to know what he's doing to me and wanting him there with me.

"Not yet," he commands, and I whimper, holding back, wanting so desperately to come again. "Your pussy feels so good," he whispers into my ear, and I swear he's trying to torture me.

I'm trembling all over again, heat flooding me as I can't delay the inevitable any longer. "Luca," I gasp. "Please, let me come." I'm clearly not above begging when it comes to Luca Ricci.

He doesn't laugh. Doesn't mock me for it. "Who do you belong to?" Luca grunts, and I feel my body tinkering at the edge.

"You," I whisper.

"I want to feel you come all over my cock," he grunts into my ear, and his words send me flying over the edge.

I moan his name, my insides clenching onto his cock, draining him inside of me, unable to hold back any further.

"I'm going to—" he grunts, and I keep him tight against me.

"Luca, come for me." I want him to feel what he's given me. My lips move to his ear, gently tugging the lobe, and I feel his cock swell as he finally reaches oblivion with me.

———

Sometime during the night, I stir.

Luca is sound asleep beside me, his arm draped across my waist.

Quietly, I climb out of bed, grab the clothes I borrowed yesterday and step out into the hallway.

He doesn't so much as budge, and I don't want to wake him. I do, however, need to use the bathroom, and he's dead asleep. I should have asked him where it was yesterday; instead, I was too busy practically setting a fire to his bed.

An amazing fire that stoked something wild inside of me.

I still can't believe we had sex! And it was fucking amazing.

Outside in the hallway, there's no indication which door is the bathroom, and all the hallway doors are closed.

Fuck.

Moonlight streams in through the windows above, lighting up a path along the stairs and down the hallway. I wander back down to the first floor. I remember using the bathroom downstairs, and I'm fairly confident I remember which door it was. If I'm lucky, someone left the door open.

My footsteps are soft on the marble flooring. The material is cool beneath my feet, and as I approach the bathroom door, I'm relieved when I find it left open.

I slip inside, quietly shut the door, and take my time. Just thinking about last night with Luca, gets my adrenaline pumping all over again. How am I going to fall back asleep?

From inside the bathroom, I hear a whimper nearby. I can't quite discern where the sound is coming from, but it's close.

It sounds like a puppy begging to be let out of its cage.

Do the Riccis have a dog?

I hadn't seen any signs of a dog, but maybe they don't let it run through their home. The place is swanky, and with marble flooring, they could be worried about scratches to the marble? Does marble even scratch?

I finish up in the bathroom and pause in the hallway. There's no sign of Nova's or Luca's parents.

I still don't understand why they live together under the same roof. This place is big enough for several families, but why share a home?

And what's with that bodyguard tonight who was by the back door?

None of it makes sense.

There's more whimpering.

Whining.

It definitely sounds like a puppy, which makes me miss the family dog, Scarlet, so much. She's an Australian Shepherd, the runt of the litter, at twenty-five pounds and fully grown. I begged Mom and Dad to let me bring her to college, but they're right, there's zero chance she'd be allowed in the dorms. And I definitely couldn't smuggle her in. She's too loud and whiny.

I quietly approach the closed door where the sound of the puppy is emanating.

Seeing as how big this place is, does their puppy have an entire room to herself?

I stand outside the mysterious door and press my ear to the door. The whimpering is definitely coming from inside.

Poor puppy, she probably has to be let out to use the potty. Hopefully, there will be a leash nearby. While the house does have a fenced-in yard, I don't want to risk chasing the puppy through the yard to get *her* back inside, assuming it's a girl.

I quietly turn the handle of the door beside the bathroom, praying it's not someone's bedroom and I'm about to embarrass myself.

Darkness floods through a set of stairs, and the whimpering grows more insistent.

A soft path of lights flickers along the stairs, making it so I don't need to turn on the light switch as I descend the wooden staircase.

There's a basement?

Of course, there's a basement. This house has absolutely everything.

The staircase is a spiral of wooden stairs, and I quietly take each step, careful not to trip and fall.

The whimpering grows louder, more insistent on my approach as I near the final stairs and can see a soft overhead bulb illuminating the space.

I expect to see a crate with a puppy and maybe even a dog bed or some other sign of an animal, but instead, the cage is floor to ceiling, with metal bars. A prison cell.

And it isn't a dog nestled inside whimpering, it's a child.

TEN

LUCA

I roll over in bed, my eyes flicker open for a second, getting my bearings. The room smells different, the air cooler.

I'm not at home.

Well, not at my home. I'm at my parents' home—the compound.

And the heated memories of last night come flooding back to me.

I just had sex with Harper McKenna.

I reach my arm out for her, but the bed is empty, the spot beside me still warm.

What the hell? Where did she go? Did she decide to sleep in her own room after all?

I've never had a girl leave in the middle of the night, or after sex, for that matter. I'm usually the one kicking them out if I don't want it to be anything serious. And Harper doesn't strike me as the kind of girl to sneak out.

Heavy footfalls patter outside the hallway. It's Harper, I can feel it.

I sit up in bed, swing my legs over the mattress and retrieve my clothes in the darkness. It takes a few seconds to put them back on and make sure they're not inside out or backward before I step out into the hallway.

I don't want her wandering alone in this place.

There's trouble brewing under this roof. I've lived here long enough growing up to know when they're keeping someone hostage or torturing a suspect.

My guess—torture.

Why else would they have kicked us out earlier?

And the entire reason I came home was to protect Harper. I'm not about to stop now.

It would have been nice if the reason we were locked out of the house earlier had been a surprise, like Harper had suggested. After all, they'd bought Nova a brand-new car, and sure, they could have been signing the papers for it, but I know better.

It's so much worse than that; I feel the heaviness like an anvil on my chest.

If it were up to me, I wouldn't have spent the night here. I wanted to go home, but Nova insisted we stay, and Harper didn't have the slightest idea what was going on.

I wasn't going to leave Harper alone, and while I considered camping outside her bedroom all night, her sleeping in my bed was definitely the better of the two options.

Not to mention we didn't just sleep.

We had the most amazing sex ever. At least, I thought it was fucking amazing. If Harper claims otherwise, she is most definitely lying. I know she came twice last night, and well, I'm a little disappointed there wasn't a third time, but we were both tired and fell asleep shortly after our festivities.

There will always be a next time.

I open the bedroom door and step into the hallway. There's no sign of Harper. I quietly tiptoe to the guestroom and quietly nudge open the door.

There's no sign of her.

Her bed is empty.

Just as I suspected.

Fuck.

My stomach roils, and I hurry down the hall looking for her.

Okay, where would she be?

Bathroom or kitchen would be the most logical options. Seeing as the bathroom door is shut, but the light is off, I'm going to guess the kitchen.

Shit.

Or maybe the downstairs bathroom.

Grimacing, I realize I didn't give her a proper tour upstairs, and well, logically, she probably wandered back downstairs to use the facilities. It's the only bathroom she saw, and the doors upstairs were all closed.

I try to quietly hurry down the stairs to the bathroom near the back wing of the house. The door is open, the toilet is still running, which tells me it hasn't been long since she was in there.

Where is she now?

The kitchen is just ahead, but there are no lights spilling from its vicinity.

The basement door is right beside the bathroom, and I momentarily hold my breath. No, she'd have no reason to wander down there.

I haven't stepped foot down the basement in years, since I watched a man be tortured and executed under my father's orders. He didn't so much as flinch as it happened. No, he beamed with pride, like he was made for this job.

The worst part.

I threw up in front of him, violently. I couldn't even hide the disgust from him, and he grabbed me by the lapels and told me I ought to grow a stomach for it because I would follow in his footsteps.

The hell I would.

I did everything in my power to not become him. I stayed away from my father, his men, the evil that he brought into the home, until today.

The basement door flings open, and Harper comes running out, nearly knocking into me with a child following behind. The boy is small, dirty, and wearing pajamas. He can't be much older than eight. He looks like he was snatched from his bed in the middle of the night.

Fuck.

"We have to go, now!" I tell her, grabbing her arm and dragging her down the hallway and to the back door. It's the closest exit to the house. I punch in the alarm code to disable it before pulling the door open and gesturing for Harper and the child to head outside before closing it. I grab my jacket hanging on the hook by the door and my tennis shoes. I toss my tennis shoes at her.

"Put these on." I know they're too big, but they're better than her bare feet or the heels she wore that will slow us down.

She slips the shoes on while I pull my coat around

the little boy, zipping it up to keep him warm. I dig my hand into the jacket pocket, retrieving my keys.

"It's okay," I tell him, although nothing is okay at the moment. "She's going to keep you safe."

Men will be on us in seconds if we're not quick. "There are cameras everywhere. Someone is always watching. We have only a few seconds, maybe minutes, if we're lucky."

I point to the forest where I procured wood earlier for the bonfire. "You have to run to the edge of the forest, get over the fence. Then run to the road and get help."

"What about you?" Harper asks. "You're not coming with us?"

"I'm going to grab the car. I'll be the diversion you both need to get to safety. Once you're over the fence, find a house, someone who will help. Call the police. Whatever you do, don't come looking for me."

It takes everything in me not to chase after her, protect her, keep her safe. But her best odds are with me here and her and the boy as far away as possible.

I can give her time to get to safety.

It's the best choice when the odds are stacked against us.

She grabs me and kisses me in a blaze of heated passion. The world around me melts, and while my feet are freezing, as are my extremities from the biting cold, all I feel is warmth from the taste of her lips surrounding all of my senses.

"If we survive this—" Harpers says, and I cut her off.

"*When* we survive this—" I correct her. I can't let any other thoughts exist.

"I don't want it to be *fake* between us," she says. She steals one more kiss before I have time to answer.

After what happened between us earlier, it could never be *fake*.

She grabs the little boy's hand and runs into the forest in the direction I told her to go.

I exhale a nervous breath and dart in front of the camera, making sure I'm the one who is being seen, my motions obvious and obnoxious as I head for the front of the building and toward my car.

Moreno opens the front door with Ashton right at his heel. He must have woken him up. Harper was reasonably quiet, and I made sure to silence the alarm. Ashton couldn't have woken and known what was happening on his own. Someone had to involve him, but why?

"Stop, before you get yourself killed," Moreno bellows out, and I pause at the front door of my vehicle, the keys in my hand. I contemplate jumping in and hightailing it out of there, but the wrought-iron fence isn't going to magically open. There's zero chance Moreno is going to order the guard at the gate to let me go free, not if they've realized their prisoner is missing.

And they must know, or else they wouldn't care about me sneaking off into the night.

"Hear him out," Ashton says. "He's trying to save your life."

"Save my life?" I scoff and step away from the vehicle. "Why does my life need saving?"

I'm trying to buy time for Harper so she can slip away unnoticed. Although I'm sure they've noticed her, but I don't hear them running through the forest.

Shit.

I do, however, hear the metal gates groaning as they open. Three vehicles with my father's soldiers are driving out of the compound, most certainly planning on stopping her when she gets over the fence.

Fuck.

I can't stop all of them. I'm not sure I can even stop Moreno and Ashton on my own. Not when Moreno has a weapon on his hip. I can see the glistening gun in his holster under the outside lights. At least he hasn't drawn it and pointed it at me. I should feel grateful.

"You're going to get yourself killed," Moreno warns me. "I'm trying to help you."

But I don't care about myself. I only care about Harper.

"Listen to him," Ashton says and slowly comes around to approach me.

I exhale a heavy breath. I already don't like where this is going. The front door opens, and Dante storms outside, fuming.

"Kill the girl," Dante shouts orders at Moreno. I imagine he already gave the orders to his men who drove out the front gate. "But bring me the child, alive."

"No!" I lunge for Dante, ready to kill my father with my bare hands. He's truly a monster, the worst kind imaginable, murdering an innocent girl.

Ashton holds me back.

"Think twice, son," Dante warns, snarling, unpleased with my lack of obedience. "I can have you buried right beside her."

Dante lifts his gun, un-cocking the trigger as he holds it up to my face.

"Would you honestly kill your only son, your heir to the throne?" I ask, knowing how to get inside his head. "Mom, *Nikki,* would hate you for the rest of your life."

He stares at me, taken aback by the mention of her name. He seems slightly puzzled, almost befuddled by the realization that I may be right. He shakes the cobwebs from his thoughts away as quickly as they come. "You've never wanted this," he says and gestures to the compound, his paradise.

"I never wanted to become *you*," I say. Although, in truth, I don't want any of his life or to be a part of the horrible things he's involved with. That's not who I am.

"Consider your options, Luca," Dante says. "Kill the girl, or if you refuse to obey, which I know you love to do, then your buddy Ashton has orders to kill you both." Dante hands over his gun to Ashton, giving him the opportunity to execute me if need be.

I glance back at Ashton.

He wouldn't?

"Sorry," Ashton says and shakes his head. He doesn't lift the gun or threaten me with it, but it's in his hand, pointed down toward the ground, and that's enough for me to know that he's on *their* side. He's taken the weapon, he's accepting the power they're granting him.

I scoff and push Ashton as I step backward. "We're brothers," I say, grinding my teeth. We may not be biological or blood, but I thought our friendship and being teammates meant something.

"You know mafia family always comes first," Ashton says.

I've always known Ashton was close to his father. I've heard the phone calls. I'm well aware that he intends to run the Chicago Bratva after college. I just didn't see him betraying me and siding with my father.

"Don't do this," I say, hoping to talk some sense into my friend.

"Don't make me pull the trigger," Ashton says as he grabs me by the shirt and shoves me toward my car. "Now, help us find Harper before she gets the child killed."

I climb into the driver's seat rather quickly. Stalling isn't going to help Harper. There are too many of them chasing her down. Her best option is my help.

Ashton, however, is going to be a thorn in my side when I finally get to her.

The iron gates remain open, and I drive onto the main road and turn left, the direction that I know she ran with the little boy.

I turn off the radio, open the windows, and feel a blast of cool air. I'm listening for any indication of a struggle, in case I don't see her but I hear her.

"You can't save her," Ashton says, the gun still in his grasp as it rests on his lap.

"Well, I'm not about to shoot her." I glare at him before returning my attention to the road. I'm following along the fence line. The property extends quite a bit, but there's no sign of her. There are several of my father's men in suits scouring the perimeter.

It's still dark outside, which is the one advantage that she'll have, the cover of night.

"She's just a girl, one who is easily replaceable," he says.

I scoff at his suggestion. "Everyone is replaceable, according to the mafia."

Ashton shrugs as his gaze peers out the window, taking everything in, looking for *her*. "You're not wrong," he says. "But don't get yourself worked up over her. She's cute and all, but she's not worth your life, and you heard Dante. He'd have me end both of you if it comes down to it. Don't be stupid, Luca. As your friend, I'm telling you to not be stupid."

My stomach sours. "Glad you're not the one who ended up with her," I mutter.

"Are you serious?" Ashton shifts in his seat.

Shit, he heard me. Not that it matters. His head is so far up the mafia's ass, apparently, he'd do anything to appease them, including killing me when the time comes.

"You are *fake dating* her. Don't forget that, Luca. It's *fake.*"

Except what happened last night between us wasn't fake, nothing about it was pretend.

I can still feel her body nestled under me, and I wish that we were both back upstairs in my bedroom. Unfortunately, I can't wind time backward or change the course of the night's events after our romp in the bedroom.

All I can do is vow to protect her.

"You wish it were fake," I grumble and slam on the brakes when I witness two men throwing the little boy into the back of their SUV parked across the street.

I hightail it out of the car, and Ashton is right on my heel.

"Harper!" I shout, glancing in the vehicle, but the windows are dark. It's nighttime and too hard to see through the glass.

But I don't hear her voice, her screams, her pleas for help.

"Where is she?" I lunge at Nico, one of my father's men, and land a blow to his face. My hands are on his shirt, demanding answers, as a trail of blood drips from his nose.

Ashton yanks me backward, off the soldier.

She wouldn't have left the boy alone. "If you killed her, I swear to—"

Matteo steps around the opposite side of the vehicle. He's calm. A little too calm, which has my heart racing erratically. I've never liked Matteo. He tortures men for a living. His only goal is to extract information before their death. "Bruno and Vito caught her trying to get over the fence. She's on her way back inside the complex," Matteo says.

"Fuck!"

ELEVEN

LUCA

There are four men on Harper, two restraining her, Halsey and Caden, and two watching to make sure she doesn't escape, Bruno and Vito.

Do they really need four men to keep her contained? It's overkill.

Nico and Matteo join the party, dragging the boy back into the dungeon, opening the cell and tossing him inside.

There's a cot on the floor and a blanket that looks worse for wear. The little boy runs toward the cot against the far wall and curls up, keeping his distance as best he can.

But Harper isn't in a cell, and knowing he wants her dead has my stomach churning. I don't question why he hasn't killed her yet. It's probably to torture me.

What the fuck is Dante involved in this time?

Matteo stands in front of Harper, his hands bunched into fists at his sides.

"Tell me why you were snooping and I won't make this unpleasant for you."

The air rushes out of my lungs.

He's talking about torture, quietly threatening her with it.

"I swear, I thought I heard a puppy!" Harper cries out, trying to wrestle the men free, but they force her into a chair.

She's not physically restrained, except for the firm hands on her shoulders by the capo, keeping her from getting up and running.

Her breathing is erratic.

I know the feeling, horror, seeing what men are capable of, and worse, it's my own father behind this child's abduction. I never knew him to traffic children, but he's a monster, always has been. And I don't know all the dirty details of his business endeavors.

"Just let the child go," Harper rasps. "I don't care about me. Do whatever you want to me."

"Oh, you'll care," Caden says with a deep, throaty laugh. "You'll beg us to kill you. Stupid girl, coming down into the mafia basement and stealing our property. You must have a death wish."

"Mafia?" Harper gasps. Clearly, she hadn't figured it out until he spelled it out for her. I'm not sure if I should be relieved that she's naïve, or embarrassed that she couldn't get there on her own.

"Let her go!" I shout. My voice reverberates against the metal bars and dulls over the stone walls.

I shove Bruno and Vito backward, out of the way so that I can get to Harper.

Bruno grabs my arm, yanking me toward him, whipping out his gun and shoving it against my temple. "And your father always thought you would grow up to be a smart man," Bruno hisses against my ear.

"Silence!" Dante shouts, and his footsteps are heavy when they tread over the cement basement floor as he approaches from down the stairs.

"What do we have here?" Dante asks, examining the girl seated in front of him. He walks around her like a lion stalking their prey. While he's aware of the crime on camera, he wants to hear it firsthand and understand his enemy.

Halsey speaks first, his grip still firm on Harper's shoulder as he keeps her positioned in the metal folding chair, facing the prison cell. "Caught the girl snooping."

"I wasn't snooping!" Harper shouts and shoves the man off her arm, but she doesn't rise from the chair. She seems to know better than to run again. Besides, the men towering above her have guns.

"What were you doing?" Dante asks, awaiting an explanation, although I can't imagine any answer would satisfy him.

"I heard a puppy, and I went to find it so I could let it out to the bathroom. Is that so horrible?" Harper asks. She doesn't even mention that she stumbled into the mafia den and found a child, then proceeded to attempt an escape with him. No sense in reminding him of what happened.

"Well, what do you suggest we do now that you've found your dog?" Dante stares coldly at Harper, waiting to hear her explanation.

"It's a child!" Harper reiterates, gesturing to the kid behind bars. "Whatever he did, he's a kid. You can't just kidnap children for the hell of it."

"Oh, believe me, I get no enjoyment from this," Dante says, his voice calm, far too calm.

I step forward, shoving Bruno backward and off me. Seeing as how my father is in the room, he doesn't rough handle me like I know he wants to. He's cautious around Dante because, after all, I am my father's son.

"I don't believe you," I say. "You've murdered men; I've seen it myself firsthand."

Dante's brow furrows. "I've murdered no one," he says, glowering at me. "Son, what you've convinced yourself you've seen, it's all—not true."

Of course, he'd balk at the suggestion that I

witnessed a crime, a murder, no less. I wouldn't expect him to admit it, not to me, not to anyone.

"And what about this? How do you explain you kidnapping a child?" Harper asks. The girl doesn't know when to keep her mouth shut.

Dante steps closer and leans down, his face mere inches from Harper's. "The way I see it, you kidnapped him from me. I'm merely protecting the little rascal. Someone should look after the child. I wouldn't want him to end up in harm's way, would you, dear?" Dante asks. He stands properly and glances back over his shoulder at the boy.

Behind me, another set of soft footsteps make their way downstairs, and it's Moreno.

Looks like a family reunion, except we're missing a few soldiers my father commands.

"Sir, I'll take care of this," Moreno says, allowing my father to return to bed if he so chooses.

Moreno is his second in command. Dante trusts Moreno with his life and with the job.

Dante glances at Moreno and then at me. "The girl is

a problem, one you both brought into my home, under my roof."

Is he blaming his second for this?

"I couldn't have known she was coming, sir. I had the other girls who had intended on attending Nova's birthday party rescind their invitation—it was without my knowledge that this girl, your son's girlfriend, would attend," Moreno says.

He's clearly covering his own ass and his family.

I shouldn't be surprised. Throw me and Harper under the proverbial bus.

Just fucking great.

I glance at Bruno's gun. I could attempt to wrestle it from his grip, but we're outnumbered and surely outmatched. I could fight one, maybe two guys, but there are six men, all fully trained, mafia style.

"Yes," Dante says, nodding slowly, stroking his jaw as he turns to face me. "This problem, it seems, is between my son and me."

Harper's head is turned, her gaze on me. I can see the cogs turning, her wondering what exactly all of this means and how the hell do we get out of this basement, alive.

"You're absolutely right, Father." It pains me to call Dante my father, but right now, I'll do whatever it takes. If I need to put on a show, perform an act, I'll give it my all. I just hope Harper has the same acting skills and will play along. Is there another way out of this disaster?

Dante exhales heavily through his nose. "Is that so?" He seems surprised, as shocked as I am, that I'm admitting he's right.

The man basks in his glory, but I'll only let him have this win for a brief moment.

"I shouldn't have brought my girlfriend here uninvited," I say. I take a moment, gathering my thoughts before continuing, hoping that what I spin will work to save her, to save both of us. "She had no idea what this place is, who you are, until one of your men, Caden, spelled it out for her, like an imbecile."

Dante's eyes tighten for a moment, and he turns toward Caden and the other men who work for him. "Is this true?"

Halsey is the first to nod. "Yes, sir." He and Caden are of equal rank. Vito works for Caden, I can't imagine he'd sell out his boss, and Bruno, well, he's Bruno. He'd sell out his own sister if given the opportunity. As would Matteo, who also agrees with what just transpired.

Dante grabs Bruno's gun and lifts the barrel. He pauses only slightly, removing the extra bullets before turning the pistol and handing it to Harper. "You kill him, and you can live."

"Excuse me?" Harper's eyes widen.

"Sir," Caden's voice wavers, "that isn't necessary. I swear I'd never betray you, sir. What I said, it was entirely an accident. I mean, I never meant to tell the girl we're mafia. It just slipped out. You know I would never—" He's babbling and pleading for his life.

Dante holds a hand up to silence Caden. He doesn't wish to hear another word from his lips.

Caden takes it as a peace offering. I'm sure he's hoping, mentally pleading, for his life. After all he's a capo, one of the men higher in rank that the soldiers. He gives orders, he's valuable and trusted, but once trust is broken, there is no apology that can mend the broken bonds of blood.

Dante gently guides his arm to Harper, having her stand and face Caden. "Shoot the traitor," Dante says into her ear, his whisper loud enough for everyone to hear. "Prove your loyalty and alliance to the family, to my son, and you both will live. You have my word."

The gun in her hand trembles as she slowly raises it, shaking her head no. Her whole body is trembling, her breaths uneven and gasping for air. She's probably having a panic attack. I sure as hell am on the brink of one as I try to protect her the only way I know how.

I step between Caden and Harper. I can't have her make that choice. She's not a cold-blooded killer.

"She's not shooting anyone," I say, stopping the insanity that is my father's game.

There's a look of relief that crosses her face as she lowers the gun and I take it in my hands. A part of me wants to raise the weapon, point it at my father, and pull the trigger.

But what then?

I don't wish to lead the mafia, and I'd be the man I despise, just like my father, but so much worse.

I turn to Dante. "Harper is under my protection. You cannot touch her."

He huffs under his breath and tilts his head. "What makes you think you can stop me, son?"

Ashton glances at my father, waiting for the command to murder both of us. Like his finger is itching on the trigger, and he's eager to have two kills to his name.

"A marriage alliance," I breathe, exhaling heavily, praying that this works. "If she's wed to me, then she's part of the family. Protected."

"But you don't wish to be mafia, Luca," Dante says, reminding me of my betrayal to the family. His gaze moves to Ashton, and he nods, as though he's giving him permission to kill both of us. "Your idea is lacking creativity." He's fucking mocking me.

I inhale sharply as Ashton raises the gun on Harper and cocks off the safety.

"Wait!" I step between Harper and the gun. "I'll come work for you."

Dante holds a hand up to Ashton, indicating for him to wait a moment before pulling the trigger.

"You'll work for me, and you'll marry her," Dante says, indicating that both options must happen.

Harper's brow furrows, and she shakes her head. "You can't dictate my life. Either of you!"

"Know when to shut up!" Dante scolds her.

"Your son is a phenomenal hockey player. You're just going to let him ruin his chances at a promising professional career after college?" Harper doesn't seem to know how much my father hates hockey. He hates all sports unless there's betting involved, and he's making money as a bookie.

Dante laughs darkly and rubs the bridge of his nose. "Your girlfriend is a real spitfire," he mutters.

Dante's eyes narrow as he steals a glance from Harper to Moreno. It's like he's looking for feedback, which is quite unlike my father.

Moreno leans in, whispers something to Dante, before standing firm.

"You are both to remain under this roof until the wedding. I can't risk *her* getting anyone else killed."

I exhale a nervous breath as Ashton begins to lower his weapon.

Dante continues; he's not done speaking. "And as for the family business, you will begin training every weekend that you do not have hockey practice or a game. You are expected to join us upon graduation, unless you are drafted by the NHL. At which point, when your hockey career ceases, you will then be expected to come and work for the family."

"Those terms are acceptable," I say in agreement, without so much as looking at Harper.

I'm doing this to save her life; she has to realize that's all that I want. To protect her.

My father turns and faces Harper. "If you give me any more problems, don't think I won't have my men torture and kill you. You are never to step foot in this room again. Is that understood?"

Harper glances at me before nodding. "Yes, sir."

"Good, she's learning," Dante says with a smirk. "You both can return upstairs to bed, but do not disappoint me."

I grab Harper's hand and lead her up the basement stairs and around the house, back upstairs. "I don't want to be alone," she whispers, and I nod and put a finger over my lips, warning her to be quiet.

I grab both of our bags and bring them to the guest quarters bathroom, flip on the light and fan, and gesture for her to join me inside. I close the door behind us.

She opens her mouth to speak, and I hold up a finger and start the shower, making sure any sound is entirely drowned out by all the noise around us.

Only now do I feel it's safe to talk.

TWELVE

HARPER

"What are we going to do about the little boy in the basement?" I ask, staring at Luca.

I shiver, the steam from the shower warming up the bathroom, but I'm still freezing from running around outside in the middle of the night.

Or maybe it's the adrenaline that's still firing through me.

Luca removes his shirt and then strips out of his pants, kicking them out of the way. He pulls back the shower curtain. "Join me."

He's not answering my question.

He hurries into the shower and steps under the hot spray.

Sighing, I strip out of his clothes that I'm wearing and join him. "Happy?" I ask, perturbed that he can't just talk to me like a normal person.

Luca's arms are instantly around my waist, tugging me against him under the hot water.

I exhale a breath, but I'm still shivering and on the verge of crying. None of this is fair.

"Talk to me," he whispers, his fingers moving over my back, touching and grazing every inch of my skin. His hands never cease to slow, and he keeps me close against him, which also allows us to share the water.

"Your father is the mafia?" I can't keep my voice down, and his answer is a silent nod.

"You should have fucking told me, Luca. Before I showed up here." I attempt to shove him off of me, but his hold on me only grows stronger.

"I know. I couldn't," he says, his breath tickling my neck as he rests his lips against my bare skin.

My body curls into his, seeking comfort, warmth, affection, while my heart is being tormented. I'm breaking inside.

"What are we going to do?" My voice catches in my throat, and I feel the first tears begin to surface.

Luca brings me in farther under the spray, letting the water wash away the first signs of moisture.

"We're going to plan a wedding."

I laugh darkly. "You can't be serious." He's out of his mind if he thinks we're actually going through with a wedding. "We don't even love each other." He can't tell me that he loves me, I'd never believe him. We've had sex once, last night, and yes, it was fucking amazing, but he doesn't know everything about me.

And clearly, I don't know everything about him either.

"There's time for that," he whispers, his thumb grazing my cheek before caressing my jaw. He tilts my chin up to meet his stare. "We're at least heading in the right direction."

"Are we?" I ask. "Because you've been lying to me."

"I couldn't tell you about my family," Luca says. He closes his eyes for a brief moment, clearly pained by what's happening. "You know that's not fair."

"But here we are," I say and gesture to the shower.

Luca sighs. "I only came back here to protect you."

"Thanks for not running off when I rescued the little kid," I mutter and pull back, trying to slip from his grasp.

He holds me tighter.

"That's not what I meant and you know it."

"Do I?" I ask. "Because I'm not sure what you mean. I'm not even sure who you are anymore." I step out of the shower, glancing down as the dirt swirls around the tub floor. I'm not entirely clean, all I did was rinse off, but standing in the shower with Luca isn't helping.

"I'm still me," Luca says and rinses under the spray. He grabs the shampoo bottle while I reach for a towel, drying off and trying to warm up. Already, I'm cold, but I'm not sure it isn't also his touch that I already miss. He closes part of the curtain, trying to keep the water off the bathroom floor, but I can still see his face, talk to him.

"I don't know what that means. I don't even know who you are," I say. "We've just scratched the surface of a relationship between us, and now we're talking about jumping headfirst into marriage. It's insane."

Luca rinses the soapsuds from his hair and then turns to face me. "Do you think I want to join my father after college?" he asks, staring straight into my soul. "This wasn't my great idea to come here this weekend. I showed up to protect you, Harper, and that's what I'm going to do. No matter what."

I yank the shower curtain all the way closed. I don't want to see him right now.

I know he's trying to help, but he's making it worse.

There has to be another way, another option; marriage isn't the answer. It isn't the answer—there's so much he doesn't know about me, about my life, and I can't just marry him. It's crazy.

Luca leaves the water running, but he steps out of the shower. He grabs a towel and begins to dry off while I grab my pajamas from my overnight bag.

I'm silent. I don't know what to say, what to do. Maybe we can pretend that we'll get married or fake a wedding and then find a way to escape his family.

We could transfer schools, move to another state, or even to another country.

But then there's my family. I can't just walk away from them. As it is, I usually call them on weekends, and they're probably wondering why they haven't heard from me.

It's so fucking complicated, and he doesn't even have the slightest idea how bad this could be, for all of us.

"Are you mad at me?" Luca asks. He slips into a pair of boxers and nothing else.

I try not to stare at his bare chest, but my body reacts even when I don't want it to. He's gorgeous, and he's not a bad guy; *his father is the monster.*

But he's going to become him if he joins the family business.

A muffled gunshot reverberates through the walls. My eyes widen in horror, and my hands tremble. I think I'm going to be sick. Did they just murder that innocent little boy or the man they wanted me to kill?

Tears burn my vision. "I can't—I can't do this. I can't marry you and pretend everything is okay."

Luca nods slowly and pulls me against him. "Then, you and I, we won't pretend. We'll be honest with each other. Always. Okay?"

The air leaves my lungs as I exhale a heavy sigh.

Honest.

He wasn't honest with me about his father, his family, the mafia.

"We won't pretend," I repeat, because I can get onboard with being real with Luca. I've always been genuine around him.

"Not to each other," he says, clarifying his meaning. "We might have to pretend in front of my parents and yours—"

Another sigh, and this time I open the bathroom door.

He turns around, shuts off the shower and hurries after me.

Luca is silent, but he's right on my heel. "Show me which room is mine," I say.

His brow furrows, and he leads me back into *his bedroom*. "It's not safe for you to sleep alone."

I don't argue. He's probably right. The last thing I want is one of his men to kill me in my sleep. "Fine," I say with a grumble and make my way to his bed. I pull back the bedsheets, but he's out in the hallway.

I want to ask him what the hell he's doing when he brings our bags back into the bedroom and closes the door quietly, locking it.

"No shenanigans," I say and point at the mattress.

"I wouldn't dream of it," he mutters. "I'm sure we can manage to share a bed like adults."

I glare at him, unsure what he's saying. Is he insinuating that I started this whole debacle? I may have found the little boy, but that doesn't excuse what happened. His father kidnapped a child.

I can't just let that go.

Even if it kills me, I can't let him hold a child hostage. I'm just not sure how to let the boy escape when there is surveillance throughout the entire mansion and my own life is in imminent danger.

Unless he's already dead.

Momentarily, I hold my breath, waiting as Luca climbs beneath the covers, his body nestled beside me. He's lying on his side, his arm on his pillow, staring at me.

I'm trembling.

Just thinking about all of it is overwhelming.

Luca pulls me against him, wrapping his arms around me. He's warm against my cool skin. I shiver and tremble, and he tries to ground me.

"Do you think the boy is dead?" I whisper, praying no one can hear us, but I have to ask. I need to know.

It's impossible that Luca didn't hear the gunshot while we were in the bathroom.

He shakes his head no. "It's unlikely they killed the child. That's not how my father operates," he says with a sad sigh. His hand reaches up, and he brushes my cheek with the back of his thumb.

"How do you know that?"

Luca pauses, considering my question. "I grew up here. He's brought hostages in before."

"Children?" I ask.

"Not that I recall, but I wasn't exactly involved in his operations. We shouldn't talk about it here. The walls have ears," he reminds me. He presses a soft kiss to my cheek. "Try not to worry."

He can't be serious. How can I not worry?

Tomorrow, I'll sneak out and go to the police. They'll have to help, especially when I tell them about the boy.

Luca keeps me close, his arm around my hip the entire night. I find it difficult to fall back to sleep, but I won't get out of bed. I'm too afraid to wander through the house, even to use the bathroom. It's too dangerous without Luca at my side. He's the only thing stopping his father from killing me.

Sometime between worry and dawn, I slip in and out of sleep. It's not quite peaceful, but I get a few hours of slumber.

When I awaken, Luca is still lying beside me in bed, but he's awake, watching me.

"You're really pretty when you sleep," he says and pulls me closer, his arm around my hip.

I gently pry his arm away from my body, and while I miss the warmth and his close contact, we can't pretend that everything horrible last night didn't happen.

"What are we going to do about school, our classes?" I ask. If Dante is intending for us to stay in his home until we're married, that's going to be problematic unless we're getting hitched within the next few days.

"Let me talk to him this morning and see what he says."

I exhale heavily and roll onto my back. "Okay." It's not like there are too many options, and the ones I'm contemplating can't be said within these four walls.

I climb out of bed and grab my bag, rummaging around for my clothes to wear.

"Which door is the bathroom again?" The last thing I want is to stumble into another nightmare.

Luca lies on the mattress on his back, one arm behind his head, watching me. "Third door, or you could just change in here." He grins at me suggestively.

I toss my clean bra at him. "I have to use the bathroom, and I don't want to wander into the wrong room. Can you walk me down the hallway?"

He fingers the bra and then folds it in half. "I'm going to keep this."

"Why? We're getting married. I'm sure you'll see all my clothes."

He presses his lips together, perhaps realizing I'm right. Or maybe he thinks I'm acting for whatever cameras or microphones are hiding in the house.

My breath catches in my throat.

"What?" Luca asks. He sits up in bed.

"Your family, they heard us last night." I stare at him, horrified.

"We didn't say anything—" His eyes widen at the realization of what I'm referring to. Not our discussion after the arrangement that's been made but our bedroom activities.

Luca climbs out of bed and grabs his clothes while I'm standing waiting for him to lead me to the bathroom. "We did tell them we're a couple," Luca says. "I'm sure they didn't think anything of the fact that we had sex."

"But they heard us!"

Luca smiles. "Could have heard us. And who cares? They'll all just be jealous that I can make you come multiple times."

I smack his arm, unlock the bedroom door and yank it open. "Show me to the bathroom."

He waits for me in the hallway until I'm done. After I finish, we switch places, and I wait for him to use the bathroom. He didn't bother to bring his clothes into the bathroom with him to get dressed.

"Harper," Luca's mother comes barreling down the hallway.

I inhale sharply and glance at the bathroom door, waiting for Luca to reappear. He'd better hurry the hell up.

"Dante told me the exciting news, but I have to ask, are you pregnant?"

My breath catches in my throat.

Dante is hurrying down the corridor of the hallway, coming up behind his wife. He's glaring at me and throws an arm around his wife's side. "Let's leave the two lovebirds alone, shall we?"

"I'm just trying to get to know Harper a little more. If she's going to be our daughter-in-law, I'd like to have a relationship with her. How about us girls grab lunch and a spa day this afternoon while the boys do whatever it is they do to celebrate the engagement?" Nikki asks.

My mouth is hanging agape as I glance from Nikki to Dante.

Is this a trap? Maybe she has no idea what her husband is involved in. I have so many questions for Luca.

I hear him shuffling around in the bathroom, and finally, he swings the bathroom door open.

"What do you say?" Nikki asks. "We can invite Nova, if you'd like as well."

My breath catches in my throat. Nova. Does she know about the horror of what's happening under this roof? Does she know that her father works for the mafia?

I can't exactly ask her if Nikki is going to be around. I glance at Luca, hoping he has some bright idea to save the day.

"I think a girls' day would be a good idea," Luca says, staring at me and then glancing at his mother.

Is he out of his mind?

Or maybe he realizes I'm safer with Nikki than with Dante? At least I'll be out of the prison that they call a home. Perhaps I can disappear long enough to get help for the little boy, unless I can trust Nikki.

Dante's eyes tighten, and he forces a smile. It doesn't look the least bit natural. "How about you hand me your phone, and I can make sure you have my number, in case you need anything."

"It's in the bedroom," I say and gesture toward Luca's room.

"Of course, it is. Would you get that for me, son?" he says to Luca.

"I know your phone number. I'll put it in her phone," Luca says, challenging him.

Does Dante intend to use my phone to spy on me? I can't fathom any other reason he would want me to have his number.

Nikki reaches for my arm and leads me down the hallway toward the stairwell. "Dante was telling me how you'll both be staying with us for a while, which I think is great, but you both do have classes to attend. Your education is important to us."

"Of course," I say, glad that at least Nikki seems to be reasonable. "I was hoping we might be able to just visit on weekends."

A strange look crosses her features. "Of course, Harper. Whatever you both want. I hope my husband didn't scare you into an invitation to stay here." Nikki glares at him over her shoulder. "Sometimes he can be a bit of a brute."

Understatement of the century.

I walk down the staircase beside Nikki.

Dante and Luca are right on my heels.

"Perhaps we should all go out to lunch to celebrate the engagement," Dante insists.

"We're going shopping and maybe even the spa. Do you really want to come with us to get our nails done?" Nikki glares at her husband, and he nods.

"Take Moreno with you."

"And that will guarantee Nova won't come along," Nikki says more to herself than to me. "Fine." She doesn't seem to argue with him.

We head downstairs, and I realize I only have my heels that I brought. I forgot to bring a second pair of shoes. I'm wearing blue jeans and a sweater. The shoes are a little awkward, but at least I don't have to run through the forest. Luca saved my ass with his big-ass tennis shoes.

His shoes are strewn by the back door, mine are placed nicely beside them.

I grab my shoes and coat while she shows me to another exit of the house, apparently where the garage is attached.

Luca is practically my shadow while I put my heels on. "If you need anything, call me."

I nod slowly. If he's sending me with his mother, then I'm to assume he trusts her. I reach for him, giving him a hug, hoping this won't be the last time I see him.

Nikki will keep me safe, right?

Moreno comes waltzing down the hallway, wearing his famous suit and shiny black shoes. He stops near the garage door, grabs a set of car keys hanging on the rack.

Luca's lips brush mine. I know it's for show. His mother is watching. She must think we're madly in love if we're engaged.

His breath is warm, his fingers pull me closer against him and my body instantly relaxes, momentarily forgetting the worry and pain that is torturing me from the inside.

I feel him moan, and I break apart the kiss before it goes any further.

Luca grazes his lips against my ear. "Moreno is there to keep you safe."

I'm not sure I agree with his assessment, considering the man wanted me dead less than twelve hours ago. All of those men had orders to kill me.

I'm guessing he's tagging along to make sure I don't bring up the abducted child in the basement. Or maybe he thinks I'll flee and rat out the fact he's mafia and murdered someone last night.

There has to be evidence of a body, blood, a crime scene.

While I could try to call or text the police, what exactly am I going to say? What evidence do I have? Is the child even still downstairs, or did they move him to another location?

I don't even know the boy's name. In such a rush last night, I didn't ask it. I just fled with him on foot and managed to get us both caught. I could try to look up missing persons on Google News and see if there are any local news articles.

But I have a sneaking suspicion that this boy hasn't been reported missing. I haven't seen any Amber Alerts pop up on my phone. I watch the news, listen to the radio, and there weren't any stories about kidnapped children recently.

"Be safe," he whispers and then kisses my lips. "Love you, babe." The words roll off Luca's tongue; they sound natural and not the least bit rehearsed.

"Love you, too." I force out a smile. "I'll see you later." I squeeze his hand before following Nikki and Moreno out into the garage. There are several vehicles, and he hits the button to unlock the dark sedan with tinted windows. The lights flash when he hits the button on his key fob, and I head toward the backseat.

Nikki does the same, walking around to the opposite side.

I'm surprised she's not sitting in the front seat next to Nova's father.

"You don't want to sit up front?" I ask, climbing into the backseat. I was hoping for some privacy so I could glance through my phone on the drive over.

Nikki smiles and shakes her head. "I see this guy all the time. I want to get to know my soon-to-be daughter-in-law," she says and fastens her seatbelt. "By the way, I hope you'll call me Mom."

The air rushes out of my lungs, and I force a smile.

Moreno glances in the rearview mirror, watching me as he drives. If I say something wrong, I get the feeling he'll have no regrets pulling the trigger.

"I must say, I'm surprised by the engagement," Nikki admits. She's turned slightly in her seat beside me, her attention entirely on me. "Are you sure you're not pregnant?"

"We've been careful," I say. "I promise that's not the reason we're rushing into this marriage."

She raises an eyebrow, as if I've said exactly what she wants to hear.

"Then why are you rushing this marriage?" Nikki asks, waiting for an explanation.

I don't know whether I can trust her. She seems genuine, but with Moreno seated up front, I can't exactly spill the truth to her or ask about the child being held in their basement.

Does she not know what her husband does for a living?

She must know. There are men living under her roof with them. It's not a typical marriage or family home.

Nikki tilts her head slightly, still waiting for my answer.

"I love your son," I say, hoping that's reason enough.

Nikki pushes a strand of her raven hair behind her ear. She's studying me, but I'm not sure why. Does she think I'm lying to her?

"You hardly know him. How long have you two been together?" Nikki asks. "Why rush the wedding?"

"Because when you're in love, you know it's right. Neither of us wants to wait. I know it seems rash, this decision to wed, but we're both adults."

Nikki laughs. "Hardly. You're what—eighteen, nineteen?" she guesses.

"Eighteen," I say.

"You're barely an adult." Nikki glances up front at Moreno. "What would you say if your daughter told you she was getting married?"

He clears his throat, and his jaw tightens. "This isn't about Nova," he says and shoots me a glare in the rearview mirror. It's a warning.

I'm doing what I can to convince Nikki, and she's Dante's wife. I can't even fathom how this is going to go when I have to tell my parents.

My stomach clenches with nerves, just imagining their disappointment. I tend to do that with them a lot. I fiddle with my purse on my lap, my fingers as restless as I inwardly feel.

"I love Luca," I say, and I'm surprised how convincing I sound aloud. "He's amazing. You've done a wonderful job of raising your son, and I know we're both young, probably foolish, but we want this. We both do."

Nikki shakes her head. "I'm still not convinced." She exhales a sigh. "What have your parents said when you told them the news of the engagement?"

"I haven't," I admit. "It all happened quite so suddenly."

She glances at my hand for a ring and notices the absence of any engagement band. "Tell me how my son proposed."

Moreno shifts uncomfortably in the front seat as he drives us closer to our destination. I can see the restaurant in the distance, but there are several traffic lights in the way, and we're stopped at a long red light that doesn't want to change.

"He got down on one knee." The lie glides out easily past my lips. It's not a hard one to tell. I've seen enough romance films to assume that Luca probably would have done the same.

"Without a ring?" Nikki asks, and I sigh.

"We're having it sized."

She shakes her head, not believing me. "I have access to my son's financials, Harper. You can't lie to me."

I press my lips together and nod weakly. "I'm sorry," I say, quick to apologize. "He wants to get me a ring. I told him it doesn't matter, we don't have to do anything fancy—the ring or the wedding. I'd be happy if we just went to the courthouse and exchanged vows."

She watches me for a long moment, perhaps deciding if I'm being forthcoming.

"Dante and I would be happy to provide the wedding bands if we both approve of your marriage."

I'm fairly certain Dante won't object. Nikki, however,

the verdict is still out, and my parents, I might have to wed without their blessing.

"You haven't sat down with my husband," Nikki says, a tight smile on her lips. "He is usually the one who needs convincing in these sorts of things."

"Does Luca propose to a lot of girls?" I doubt that's what she means, but I can't fathom what she's trying to say. Is she intentionally being cryptic?

Nikki laughs, taken aback by my question. "Certainly not. But Dante is a very traditional man," she says, as if that explains everything. "He will want to make sure you both share the same values before marriage."

"Like religion and politics?" I'm throwing a guess at what she's trying to say.

"Well, that too." Nikki nods and waves her hand dismissively. "We'll get into all that later. Right now, I want to hear the rest of that proposal."

Moreno pulls up in front of the restaurant. "Wouldn't it be better to hear it over dinner, with the two of them together?" Moreno asks.

It's the first time I'm grateful for his input.

Is he actually trying to help, or just keep me from having to repeat my story and flub it up with Luca offering his own set of details?

Nikki huffs while Moreno climbs out of the vehicle and walks around to open the door for her. She steps out first, and then I slide across the backseat, exiting out the same door.

"I'll meet you girls inside," Moreno says.

Not a single moment of peace. Well, maybe one or two.

Moreno shuts the car door behind us, and I head into the restaurant with Nikki, grabbing a table for two.

"Three," Nikki corrects me.

"I was hoping he'd sit at the bar," I mutter under my breath as the waitress retrieves three menus and brings us to a table in the far corner of the restaurant. Nikki sits across from me, which still feels intimate.

The place is swanky, with white tablecloths and folded cloth napkins.

I'm not particularly hungry, which has little to do with the hour and more to do with what transpired last night. But I'm going to be expected to eat. It's nearly lunch time and I had already skipped breakfast.

The menu doesn't have any prices, which tells me all I need to know. This place is outrageously expensive. I just hope Moreno or Nikki plan on picking up the tab.

I do have a credit card for emergencies that my parents gave me, so I suppose if the check gets divided three ways—yeah, I'm screwed.

"Tell me about yourself," Nikki says. "If you're not going to give me the proposal story until dinner, I want to get to know you. It's why I insisted on us girls going out today together."

I bite my tongue on the *us girls* comment, because Moreno is definitely not a girl. He's with us solely to make sure I don't fuck up.

"I'm a freshman at Evergreen. Luca and I are in the same Econ 101 class."

"Is that how the two of you met?"

I nod and reach for the water glass, taking a sip. Already, I feel parched, but at least sticking with the truth is easy.

"Yes, he kept sitting next to me in class, wanting to borrow my notes, and walking me to my next class when we finished econ."

"That's sweet." Nikki smiles, and I can feel her genuine warmth radiating toward me. "Tell me more. How did you two get from class to this?" She gestures at me, wanting more details.

"I've been struggling with some of the basic concepts in class. Luca is really smart." I don't have to lie. It's true, he's been doing so much better in our economics class than I have. "He's been helping tutor me after class. He's always able to explain everything that we learned in class in a way that I can actually understand it. I swear, he should be a professor. We started having these study sessions, just the two of us—"

"Oh?" Nikki raises an eyebrow and holds up a hand. "I don't need the sexual details. Please leave those out."

I can't help but laugh. Nothing sexual happened at our study sessions, but maybe her thinking it did helps make it more believable. I smile shamelessly and twirl a strand of my hair, trying to act flirty as I pretend to think of Luca in a sexual manner.

Which isn't really that hard after last night. Just remembering his lips kissing every inch of my body and his cock driving me crazy is enough to stir the feelings buried deep within me.

After a second, I laugh, hoping that maybe my flushed cheeks help her believe the story. "Well, then I'm sure you get the idea. We studied, he helped me pass the exam. Honestly, Luca is a really great guy. He's the absolute best and he makes me happy."

All universal truths.

He does make me happy.

Most of the time.

Moreno comes waltzing in, and I realize the time to have asked her anything personal and secretive is long over. Damn, I should have been the one in control.

"What'd I miss?" Moreno asks as he grabs a seat at the table next to me.

"Just us girls discussing Harper's love life." She winks at me, and I suppress a groan. "So, I'm assuming you've been to his hockey games. Are you a sports fanatic?" Nikki asks. "You know how much my son loves hockey."

"I wasn't really into sports growing up, but Luca seems to be changing that. I went to my first hockey game this semester."

Definitely not a lie. Although I didn't exactly stay through the entire game. It was brutal watching Luca get his ass kicked. I don't want to worry Nikki, though, so I stick to the basics.

"What did you think?" she asks, wanting my honest opinion.

"It's a brutal sport." Another easy truth. No one can say hockey is gentle.

Nikki laughs. "Agreed. But there's been no stopping him from playing. He's been in skates since he was four."

"Wow." I'm surprised that he's been interested that long. I've never asked him about hockey, mainly because I hate sports and I really didn't think we'd become anything more than friends.

"Who got him into hockey?" I ask.

"Definitely not my husband." Nikki forces a laugh, and Moreno rolls his eyes.

"Dante hates hockey," Moreno says, joining in the conversation.

"He doesn't love the idea of his son getting hurt," Nikki says, defending her husband. "I took him ice skating as a kid, and he loved it. Luca had a natural talent for the ice, and he saw some kids playing ice hockey on the way home from the rink. He was six at the time and thought it looked like a lot of fun. He begged us to sign him up."

"Dante wasn't pleased," Moreno says, his face grim. "But Luca begged to play as his Christmas present and, well, he'd give the boy anything."

I wonder if the same Dante is still inside that cold, calculated monster. Was he mafia back then, or did he join when Luca was a child?

That's not a question I ask Moreno or Nikki.

"Dante still isn't thrilled with Luca playing hockey. He just worries that his son is going to get hurt," Nikki says.

Moreno glares at her. I get the feeling there's more to it than mere concern for his overall health, but I don't push the issue. I know better when Moreno is involved. He isn't about to help me.

"Enough about Luca. I would have thought he'd have told you that," she says and sizes me up. "So, you don't care much for sports. Did you ever play any sports as a kid?"

"Does bowling count?"

That gets a slight chuckle from both Moreno and Nikki.

I never thought I'd see Moreno lighten up, but I suppose even bad guys can laugh once in their life.

The waitress comes over and we order lunch. I'm relieved for the break in questions. It feels like a very mild interrogation. Which isn't a surprise, since I was invited to join Nikki alone for lunch.

But we're not very alone, considering Moreno has joined us. Why couldn't we have let Luca come too? It would at least make the experience a little more enjoyable.

I keep thinking about that boy in the basement. Nikki seems nice enough, but I'm not sure if I can trust her.

I excuse myself to the bathroom, taking my purse with me. It's only a few feet from our table, and I relish the fact that it's a single-occupancy restroom and I can shut and lock the door.

I don't actually have to go. I just need a break from all the questions. I reach into my purse, digging around for my phone.

It's not in there.

Did Luca grab my phone to put Dante's number in it and forget to give it back to me?

Crap. I don't think I grabbed it from upstairs before leaving. Well, there goes any chance of trying to get help for the boy.

Grumbling, I can't even try to search for information on the missing child. I glance around the bathroom. There's a paper towel that I could use to write on, perhaps leave a note for someone to help, but I search and there's no pen in my purse, either.

I usually carry a pen with me.

Weird.

Did someone go through my belongings before I left the house? I feel weirdly suspicious, but it could just be a coincidence. Maybe I used the pen and I forgot to put it back with my things.

I finish in the bathroom and step out, coming back to the table. Nikki and Moreno are having a friendly chat about me, it seems.

"I was just telling Moreno how nice it is to meet a girlfriend of Luca's. He's never brought any girls home before. We should invite your parents to join us for dinner next weekend."

"Next weekend?" My voice catches in my throat.

I'm not ready to tell my parents about Luca or the engagement. And doing it all within the next several days is dizzying. I reach for my water glass, needing another sip.

"Yes, unless they have plans already. Then we can try for the following weekend," Nikki insists. "I'm sure they have some time free. I would imagine they'd like to get to know the family their daughter is marrying into." Nikki says those words with a warm smile, but I can't help but wonder how much she knows.

Moreno stares right through me. "She's right; it would be nice for our families to meet, to get to know one another."

I don't know why, but I feel as though that's a threat, him wanting to meet my family. He's already made it clear that if I don't wed Luca, I'm dead.

The last thing I want is to put my family in harm's way. They've done nothing wrong. "I'm not sure they'll be pleased with our engagement," I admit.

"Something we both agree on," Nikki says, staring at me. "But I do like you, Harper. You seem like a good person. I just wish you and my son would wait a little while longer before jumping into marriage."

How can I tell her that this wasn't my idea? And while it may have been Luca's idea, it had been done solely to protect me.

He doesn't want to marry me.

How could he? We're both still in college. We barely know each other. We've only scratched the surface and haven't even been out yet on our first real date.

We had plans to do that this weekend after I returned from Nova's birthday party. I'm not sure when I'll be allowed to leave.

When I don't say anything, Moreno finally speaks up.

I don't have the slightest idea what words will spill from his lips, but he stares at me and nods. "She's following her heart."

"You approve of their engagement?" Nikki asks, staring pointedly at Moreno. "You wouldn't feel that way if it were your daughter."

"Nova isn't getting married," Moreno states matter-of-factly. "This isn't about *her*."

It's almost as though I'm not seated at the table, and quite frankly, that would be fine. I'd be happier to just let them talk about me than have to defend the reasons that I'm marrying Luca.

Moreno kicks me under the table, and I cough, reaching for my water glass.

Is he always this much of an asshole? Nova never mentioned her parents, at least not in any violent aspect. Then again, neither did Luca.

I take a sip and then glance between the two of them. "Is this what I have to look forward to, my parents bickering when we announce our engagement?"

Nikki laughs. "We're not married." She's quick to remind me that they're not a couple.

Yeah, well, Luca and I are barely a couple too. Look how that's turning out. I hold my tongue and keep from saying the wrong thing.

"Nikki is just concerned that you're marrying her son for the wrong reasons," Moreno says, glaring at me.

"Don't put words in my mouth," Nikki scolds him.

The woman is a bit of a spitfire.

Turns out, I like her.

Maybe we can get along. If she talks to Moreno this

way, I can only imagine the tongue on her that she has around her mafia husband.

The waitress brings our food to the table, and I stare at my pasta, my stomach churning. I can't eat. The smell of the food is overpowering, and I excuse myself, hightailing it for the bathroom again.

But this time I hear Nikki as I hurry away. "Are you sure she's not pregnant?"

I'm definitely not pregnant. It's been twelve hours since Luca and I fell into bed together. We used a condom, I'm on the pill, and pregnancy symptoms don't occur that fast.

No, this is one hundred percent a panic attack because I'm being forced to marry a man whose father runs the mafia.

I turn the sink water on and stand over it, my hands gripping the porcelain as I stare down at the rushing water.

Gasping for breath, I'm trying to slow my breathing, my heart rate, and the million thoughts and fears swimming through my head.

It's not just my life that's getting fucked up.

I really wish I had my phone so I could text Luca. He's the only person who understands what I'm going through. He's experiencing it too.

I'm not alone.

Except, right now, I feel that way, completely, utterly overwhelmed. I rinse my face with the cold water, hoping my rosy cheeks will return to their regular hue.

I feel hot, clammy, and nauseous.

But I don't think I'm actually going to vomit.

It's just the fear riding through me like an electric current with nowhere to escape. I'm burning inside, and not in the fun, tingly, I'm aroused type of sensation. This one pricks at my skin, my muscles, firing pain signals all the way from my brain to my toes.

Everything hurts.

It's bloody agony, and they haven't done anything to me.

The mafia hasn't touched me physically. Sure, they restrained me last night, threatened to kill me, but I'm without actual scars.

Emotionally, however, I'm a disaster.

How am I going to explain this to my parents? They're never going to accept Luca, certainly not after knowing him for a semester.

And his parents? I'm afraid to introduce my family to them. What if they see through the horror and realize the monsters that lurk in the shadows will become my family?

They're not going to accept Luca if they have any inkling of what's going on.

And even if they don't and all goes smoothly, there's little chance they'll be happy with the news of our engagement.

I can fake a lot of things, but pretending to be excited for a wedding neither of us wants, they'll see through it.

There's a soft knock at the bathroom door.

"Someone's in here!" I shout.

"Are you okay in there?" Nikki asks through the door.

No, I'm not the least bit okay. But I can't tell her that, not with Moreno staring me down at the restaurant table. I consider my options; none of them are ideal, and finally, I open the bathroom door, letting her inside with me.

"I'm having a panic attack," I confess, staring up at her, praying she won't push and ask me why.

She reaches for my hands, bringing them to her own. "Why are you panicking?" she asks, her voice calm, steady, her focus entirely on me.

It's only the two of us. I could tell her everything— about the boy in the basement, the forced marriage, her husband is mafia—but instead, I shake my head, trembling.

"I'm overwhelmed," I say.

It's the truth, but it's more of a quiet truth, compared to the real reasons I'm feeling this way.

"Because of the wedding?" she asks.

"My parents are going to freak out when I tell them. You have no idea how supportive they are, but this— it's going to break them."

Nikki nods slowly, and her breathing is soft and calm. "Breathe with me," she says, telling me when to breathe in, hold it, and exhale.

I'm struggling to breathe, my heart racing, gasping for breath.

Her hands wrap around my hips to steady me. "Let's try something else. Grounding," she says.

I nod and tremble, my insides beginning to feel like jelly.

"Name three colors that you see."

"Beige," I whisper, staring at the bathroom tile of the walls.

She nods in agreement. "What else?"

"Gray and white," I say, studying the marbling color and swirl pattern of the porcelain sink. My breathing is becoming less erratic.

"Good. Give me two more colors."

"Olive green," I say, staring at the soap dispenser, "and pink." The soap is an ugly shade of neon pink.

A smile quirks at the corner of her lips. "Therapy taught me to work on grounding myself when things get—overwhelming," she says. She shuts off the sink that's been running the entire time in the background.

There's a prominent knock on the bathroom door.

"We're fine, Moreno," Nikki shouts to him through the thick door.

"Just checking." I can imagine him grumbling and returning back to his seat at the table.

"Is there anything else bothering you?" Nikki asks.

Now is the time to tell her the truth about the boy from last night. The child locked inside a cage in the basement.

I glance up, meet her stare, but the words don't come.

She's Dante's wife, and I want to trust her, but I'm not sure she'd even be able to help me if I tried. Moreno is waiting for us.

Besides, she has to know what he's involved in; there's no way a woman as smart as Nikki isn't privy to what's happening under her roof.

We were kicked out of the house last night when I'm assuming they brought the child inside to the prison basement. I doubt they kicked her out of her own home.

Does she know about him?

She doesn't strike me as the type to get involved with the mafia. From first impressions, she seems like a decent mother, worried about her son, wanting to know why we're jumping into marriage after barely knowing one another.

But I'm reluctant to trust her.

She's married to him. She must know something. You don't live in a house with dozens of men patrolling the property without asking questions.

Or, in my case, snooping around.

Not that I was intending to sneak around and look for anything, other than the whimpering puppy I thought I heard. I guess the Ricci's don't have a family pet.

"Anything at all?" Nikki asks again, releasing her grasp on me now that I'm steady, grounded, and feeling better. "It's just the two of us."

It is just the two of us, but I can't trust her unless she trusts me first.

She hasn't given me any indication that she feels her life is in danger. She's not telling me to get away, to protect myself or Luca. I want to trust her, but I wonder if it's foolish hopefulness driving me to open my lips.

No words come.

Maybe it's better that way.

The fear making me silent, keeping me from trusting his mother.

I can't help but realize when I left today with Nikki, our entire afternoon was already planned. From the restaurant to our spa day, which I'm now beginning to regret.

Dante made sure I wouldn't be going anywhere without a mafia thug following me.

I was never asked where I wanted to eat or what type of food I'd like to grab. Moreno made the decision for us, or perhaps Dante had made it prior to us leaving.

Is that what it will be like on campus?

Moreno or another one of Dante's men making decisions for me, following me around, my constant unavoidable shadow?

"Do you think you're ready to go back out to the table?" Nikki asks when she's met with my silence.

"Yes," I whisper, hoping that I can manage to get a few bites of pasta down.

"Good. Try not to get too stressed. I know things might get a bit rough, but I promise you that I'm here for you," Nikki says.

I want to believe her, but I'm not sure I can. The only person I trust is Luca, but I can't even reach out to him because I don't have my phone.

THIRTEEN

LUCA

Nova comes barreling into me headfirst and then grabs my arm, dragging me out of the hallway and into the closet. The closet is huge, and while it was made for coats and shoes, there's a nook in the back with a stained-glass window that reaches the courtyard out back.

Natural light shines in through the window, making it so neither of us are literally in the dark.

"Are you okay?" I ask, sensing her dread. I'm just not sure what she's so worked up about.

"Where's Harper?" Nova asks, her voice catching in her throat. "I can't find her anywhere, and last night a lot of shit went down. Do you know what happened? Rhys stood outside my door and wouldn't let me leave my room." She's panicking, and I don't blame her.

I feel the panic setting in since last night, and the dread still hasn't gone away yet. I'll feel better when she's back home, well, at the very least, back here in the compound.

"She's out with Mom," I say.

"Your mom or mine?" Nova asks, her brow pinched as she's trying to process the information. "And why is she hanging out with one of our mothers?"

"My mom," I clarify and wince. I'm not sure how much to tell Nova. "Shit got really bad last night."

"Fuck." Nova's eyes shut, and she pinches the bridge of her nose. "I never should have invited her over; that was stupid of me."

I want to agree with Nova. It is partially her fault we're in this mess, but I'm not going to place the blame on her. We're all responsible.

"What's done is done," I say. We can't change the

past, no matter how much I wish it were a week ago, or even a few days ago.

"What the hell happened last night? Do you know? I heard a gunshot."

I stare at her pointedly. "We all heard it. Pretty sure it was Caden who was shot."

"A fucking capo?" Nova's jaw drops. "No way. Your dad wouldn't have ordered him executed."

"He admitted to Harper that they're mafia."

"Holy Hell," she gasps and paces the length of the closet. "Where's Harper now?"

"With my mom," I reiterate. I thought I told her that already, but she's freaking out, and I'm doing my best to keep myself calm. "Harper wandered into the prison cellar."

"No fucking way!"

I'd scold her if I didn't use the same language. "There's a bigger problem at hand."

"Bigger than Harper—oh my gosh, is she being held downstairs? No, wait, you said she's with your mom." She's trying desperately to keep up. "How did she end up going from witnessing the prison to hanging out with your mom?"

"You're going to need to sit down for this." I gesture to the bench by the window. It's wooden, not the most comfortable, but it will do.

Uneasily, she sits and clasps her hands together, but she's fidgeting.

I can feel the nervousness exuding from her, and I'm wracked with the same amount of guilt that Nova must be feeling.

"Harper heard a crying sound and wandered into the basement last night. Turns out my father is holding a little boy hostage."

"Your father is unbelievable!" Nova jumps up from her seat.

I point for her to sit back down.

"That's not all of it?"

"Do you think Harper would just go back to bed after that?" I ask.

Nova's eyes widen as she realizes something worse had to have happened. She waits for me to finish the story.

"Harper tried to escape with the boy. I attempted to help her, but she got caught by the fence line and dragged back here. The worst part, I was ordered to kill her, and Ashton had orders from my father to kill me and her if I didn't go through with it."

Nova's sitting at the edge of the bench, her hands gripping the seat. "You obviously didn't kill her."

"She's fine, mostly," I say with a heavy breath. "Dante wanted her to kill Caden. She doesn't have it in her, and I wasn't going to let her pull the trigger. So, I came up with a solution."

Nova's brow furrows. "You came up with a solution?" She's not convinced. To be honest, I'm becoming less and less convinced of the idea the more I sit with it.

"The two of us marry, I join my father's business after college, unless I can get drafted by the NHL. Then, after I'm done with hockey, I'm forced to work for him."

She rests her head in her hands, the weight of everything heavy on her.

"You're going to marry Harper?"

"I don't see another choice," I say. "You know how Dante always rattles on about protecting family. I'm making Harper part of our family."

Nova slowly lifts her head, glancing at me. "But you're damning your soul to work for Dante," she says. "You hate your father. You always swore you'd never become him, never work for him. I know you care about Harper, but maybe there's another way."

"I'll have to make sure I'm drafted into the NHL," I say. It's the only answer that gives me the chance of freedom.

"You're not alone, Luca. We'll figure this out," Nova says.

"Thanks."

"So, why is Harper with your mother?" she asks for the umpteenth time.

"Mom caught wind this morning of our swift engagement. She wants to get to know Harper and is probably doing her own brand of interrogation on her."

"That's not great news, considering your mom was

the daughter of Gino DeLuca." He was another mafia boss, now he's just a corpse.

"Yeah, but Harper doesn't know that. She didn't know this place was a mafia compound until Caden used the *m* word."

"Mother," Nova cackles.

"You know what I mean." I didn't even want to come back home. I wouldn't have if it hadn't been for Nova's birthday party.

I swallow the blame, it's mine to endure. I should have woken when Harper climbed out of bed. It was my job to keep her safe, and I failed miserably.

"What are we going to do about this boy?" Nova asks, tilting her head to the side as she stares up at me.

I like that we're on the same page. The two of us have always been allies under this roof, and while our fathers condone violence, neither of us wants there to be any more bloodshed.

Nova lost her mother and her nanny as a young girl.

I don't know how she's come to forgive her father. If Mom had perished, I'd never forgive Dante. Hell, I still don't forgive him for what I witnessed as a child.

"I can't ask Dante," I say and stare at her pointedly. "I can cause another distraction, but there are cameras, and I'm not sure my ruse will work again."

"I'll talk to my father as soon as he returns with Harper," Nova says. "Did we get the boy's name? Maybe we can do a little reconnaissance and figure out who he belongs to."

"I did not and Harper didn't mention it." I rub the back of my neck. Anxiety pricks at my skin. "I could send an anonymous tip out—"

"And get this place raided?" Nova stands and huffs. "You could get all of us killed!"

The closet door swings open unannounced, and Dante stares at the two of us having our little secretive meeting.

How much did he hear? I know better than to ask, but it weighs heavily on me.

"Nothing goes unnoticed under my roof," Dante says, his voice chill as he gestures for us to exit the closet.

Nova hurries past me, knowing not to upset the don.

I take my time, stopping at the entrance to the hallway, and stare into his icy cold gaze. "I may be forced to work for you, but I'll never trust you," I seethe.

Dante doesn't so much as flinch. "I can live with your hatred, son. I've done so for years. Your fiancée will be home any minute. Might I suggest you focus on *that* instead of whatever else you two were scheming."

I huff under my breath and brush past him, stepping out into the hallway.

At least he doesn't know what we were discussing. If he did, he'd probably throw me down into the prison cell with that child.

I ignore Dante, stalking down the hallway. Nova already hurried off, probably keeping out of my father's way. I don't blame her, she's smart. Besides, she's still living under his roof until graduation in a few weeks.

He digs into his jacket pocket, retrieving his phone, and glances at the screen. I can tell he's tracking Mom with his app, and I roll my eyes, heading for the kitchen.

I've barely had anything to eat today, my stomach doing somersaults after last night, but maybe a cup of coffee will at least keep the impending headache at bay.

I know my way around the kitchen, and while they have a personal chef, I prefer to do things on my own, my own way.

A few minutes later, I hear the commotion from the hallway as Mom and Harper join us back inside the compound.

I breathe a sigh of relief, not because I worried Mom would do anything to Harper, but Moreno was with them. The coffee is just about ready, but it'll have to wait. I hurry to check on Harper, wrapping my arms instantly around her waist.

She leans into my embrace, exhaling softly like she'd been holding her breath the entire day. I know better than to ask if she's doing okay. She begins to unbutton her coat, and I pause my hands over hers. "How about we take a walk?" I suggest, wanting the cover of privacy to talk.

"Oh, okay." Harper nods agreeably, and I slip on my coat and shoes, accompanying her out the back door into the yard. While there are cameras outside, they don't pick up on any sound.

I hold her hand as we walk, unwilling to let her go. I need to feel her to know that she's truly safe.

"How'd lunch and the spa with Mom go?" I ask.

"We only did lunch," Harper says. A heavy breath of air rushes out of her lungs.

"That well, huh?" I can sense her frustration.

We walk alongside one another through the yard and into the forest, where it at least feels peaceful. I know it's anything but that—last night she was running through here trying to escape with the child.

"Your mom seems nice, but I don't know—Moreno was with us the entire time. It definitely felt like he was there to make sure I didn't say anything to your mom about last night."

I tug her hand and stop walking. "I'm sure Mom knew what was going on."

Harper stares at me, confused. "How?"

"He probably told her," I say. "There's no way that she didn't hear the gunshot last night or the men storming the compound. Nova woke up, they had a guard outside her door."

"Oh," Harper whispers, her eyes wide. "Do you think —was it a test?" Her cheeks burn, and I can only hope that if it was, she passed it.

"Tell me what happened."

She recounts to me the events of the lunch, how my mother asked about us. None of it seems suspicious until she admits that Mom came to check on her in the bathroom when she couldn't eat lunch.

"I swear I didn't mention the little boy," Harper whispers. "I almost did, but I thought better of it."

"Good."

"What did you tell her?" I ask.

"That I was having a panic attack and was overwhelmed. Not a lie."

My heart aches hearing what Harper is going through. I pull her tighter, closer, wrapping my arms around her. Her damn coat is in the way, but I don't care. My fingers move to her cheek, caressing the soft skin as I run my fingers into her hair, pulling her lips closer to mine. "We're in this together," I whisper.

She shivers and smiles weakly. "Yeah, I know."

"Let's get you back inside if you're cold."

I escort her back into the house. It's several degrees warmer, and already I'm sweating from the sudden flux in temperature.

I strip out of my jacket and shoes, Harper doing the same.

We waltz past the kitchen, and I pause when I hear Nova's voice and catch the back of Moreno's head as we're heading in their direction. They're standing several doors down, and I yank Harper with me into the open bathroom, not wanting to interrupt them.

I hold a finger over my lips, gesturing to remain quiet and still.

"Since when are you in the business of kidnapping children?" Nova asks, glaring at her father.

FOURTEEN

NOVA

It's impossible to live under the roof of the mafia and not have an inkling of what's going on. You'd have to be absolutely stupid.

I've lived in this same house all my life, or at least all that I can remember.

My mother died when I was a child, the memories still vivid, but with flashes of blood that blur the lines of reality encased in trauma.

Years of therapy when I was a kid helped me unpack some of it, but of course, the therapist wasn't your average shrink.

She worked for my father, Moreno Ricci.

Trust is one of those things that, once it begins to crumble, can never be perfectly whole again. And while I trust my father, I don't trust him implicitly.

I know he does bad things.

He's not a good man, but he's been good to me.

He brought Paige into my life; my stepmother, who helped me through the losses and made me realize that my father isn't a monster, he's just a man.

Which makes it easier for me to stand up to him, even if it's foolish and stupid.

"I can't believe you!" I seethe, practically growling at him.

I made sure no one else is around when I would begin my own interrogation.

He stands there, staring at me, waiting for me to elaborate.

"You sound just like your mother," he says, his tone soft, but it strikes a chord within me, and I suspect it does him as well.

I don't ask if he means my stepmom Paige or my biological mother, whom I barely remember. The only memories I carry of her are the gruesome ones of her murder.

"That's not fair," I say. He's trying to disarm me emotionally. I'm not some little kid who runs around this place with their head in the clouds.

I see what's happening, and I know far more than I let on. I've also learned silence keeps me out of trouble. One reason I was mute as a little girl. If I couldn't say anything, I couldn't be harmed.

At least, I held that belief strongly until I realized my father would do anything to protect me, to protect the family.

Dad works for Dante. He takes orders, always obeys; it's what makes him a great second in command. And if something happened to Dante, Dad would probably fill the role.

Which would be fine. I'm not rooting for Dante to kick the bucket, but I also hold no disrespect for my father. I know who he is. I learned it at a young age, so young that I don't remember a time before.

To me, he's always been mafia, before I even knew what the mafia itself was or meant.

Dad looks at me with curious eyes, but he doesn't say anything. He's waiting for me to speak or to walk away. I'm sure he's silently praying that I'll walk away, but that's not the daughter Paige raised.

"Since when are you in the business of kidnapping children?" It's like steam is emanating from my body, and I can't stop myself from demanding an answer.

His eyes warn me to be silent, but I can't just back down when I've heard there's a little boy being held against his will. "Nova." His tone is all he needs with the use of my name, and he's telling me to back down.

No, I won't.

I open my mouth, and he grabs me by the arm and drags me into the cellar.

"Oh, fuck no," I mutter, trying to break free. "What the hell?" I can't believe my own father would betray me.

"Quiet, or you'll get us both killed," he grits between clenched teeth. We hover on the stairs and he stalks down, making sure there are no guards in the basement. There's no need with the prison cell locked tight.

My eyes widen when I see the child, and my heart physically aches for him. "You're a fucking monster!"

"Language!" Dad isn't pleased with my words, and well, I'm not the least bit pleased by his actions.

"You're worried about my language? How could you kidnap a child?" I gesture to the boy in the basement.

"We're not kidnapping per se."

"Are you trying to rationalize what you've done?" I can't believe him. I tug away from his grasp, not trusting that he won't throw me behind bars next. For knowing too much, for saying something, for disobeying him, the reasons are endless.

He's mafia, and I'm just the daughter of the second in command.

I'm a no one to them, but I suspect if something happened to me, Paige would never forgive him. That's the one thing I do have going for me. My stepmom loves me as much as she loves him.

"I don't answer to you," Dad says.

"Please, help me." The little boy behind bars steps forward into the light.

The area is dimly lit, but it's clear he's still wearing his pajamas.

"Did you kidnap him from his bed?" I'm appalled and disgusted.

"We're just protecting the family," Dad says. He doesn't flinch, but I know my father. He'd never hurt a child, but he would exact revenge for a child who's been harmed. I stare at the little boy, wondering if someone harmed him, but if they did, why would Dante have ordered the child withdrawn from his home and locked in a cage?

"Right, because this kid is a solid threat to the foundation of your organization."

"His father is, Nova, and that's all you need to know."

"Tell me how," I say, staring at him, begging for his help. "You can't just leave the kid in here forever, and what's your plan after you've what—axed his father?"

"I don't owe you answers."

"You owe me for Mom's death." I stare at him callously.

His eyes glaze over with anger or sadness; I'm not quite sure. "That's enough, Nova. Just know we're doing what is necessary to protect *children*." It's with such certainty in his voice, his conviction that he believes he's doing right.

"How long until he's released?" I ask. "You can't keep him locked up, and I swear if you have any intention to harm a hair on that child's head—"

Dad smiles at me. "You'll what?" He tilts his head, amused by my threats. "I never thought I'd say this, but you might actually join the family business someday."

"Over my dead body," I scoff at his suggestion.

"Don't be so melodramatic, Nova, you would actually be pleased with our mission."

"Kidnapping a child?" I shake my head and stalk closer to the prison cell. "Are you okay? Do you need food, water, a blanket?" I ask, ignoring my own flesh and blood.

"He's fine," Dad shouts at me.

The little boy shrugs.

"What's your name?"

Dad's voice reverberates through the prison cell. "Tell her, and I'll kill you myself."

The child slinks back to the corner of the cell.

"You're a monster," I growl at Dad and begin to stomp up the stairs.

He grabs me by the arm, yanking me back down the two stairs that I've made it up. "And you're going to get us both killed if they know I've said anything to you. Do you have a death wish?"

"I'm not afraid of dying," I say, staring him cold in the eyes. "I stopped being afraid when I watched my loved ones die in front of me."

He exhales sharply. "I'm sorry you witnessed that, Nova."

Dad steps closer, his hand reaching out to touch me, and I balk, keeping out of his reach. It's not that I'd usually believe he'd hurt me, it's that he has a child imprisoned, and I'm beginning to wonder if I really know my father at all.

FIFTEEN

NIKKI

Lunch goes about as well as can be expected. I'm a bit relieved we end up cancelling our afternoon spa appointment because I don't think Harper and I could handle another couple of hours together.

"You're home, kitten," Dante says, greeting me as soon as I'm in the door. His hands are all over me, his breath tickling my neck, and I swear the more I'm away, the more the man craves my company.

He helps me out of my coat, and I slip out of my shoes, following him down the hallway to his office.

Dante has his arm snaked around my waist as he pulls me into his private escape and shoves me against the door, slamming it shut behind us. His mouth is fused to mine, his tongue parting my lips, and I willingly oblige.

Nearly twenty years together, and this man still makes me weak at the knees. His lips pepper my skin, trailing down my neck, and I feel warmth flood through my body.

"Dante," I mumble half-coherently as I try to focus on why we're actually in his office.

It has nothing to do with sex, but somehow, we always forget that when it's the two of us alone. It's no wonder we only ended up with Luca and not a dozen children, but I'm grateful for the one I have.

"Tell me everything." Dante kisses his way down my breasts, and my fingers tangle in his thick, dark hair as I pull his face back up to reach mine.

"She won't betray the family," I say, certain that I've spent enough time with her to know the truth.

"Are you sure?" Dante questions, his brow pinched as he pulls away from our heated exchange of kisses.

"She's conflicted, that much is obvious, but she won't mention what she saw last night or the boy, and I gave her the opportunity to tell me in private. You aren't to harm a hair on her head," I warn him.

A crooked grin crosses his features. It's rare to see him smile, but I love it when he lets down his guard to let me inside. "Are you giving me orders, kitten?"

"I'm telling you that if you hurt her, our son will never forgive you."

Dante pulls back and folds his arms across his chest. He crosses his legs as he leans back on the desk, considering my words. "There are other girls."

"I haven't spoken with Luca alone, but I suspect he loves her, and it's obvious she cares deeply for him. You heard the two of them last night—"

Dante chuckles. "Who didn't? But sex is just that— you and I were fucking long before we fell in love. He will find another girl if I choose to call the order."

"You make that command, and you'll be choosing a new wife," I threaten.

Dante's gaze tightens, and he steps closer to me once again. "Are you threatening me, kitten?"

"I'm reminding you that you almost lost your son

once. You order the hit, and you will lose him forever."

He lets out a soft sigh and turns away. He's considering his words, or perhaps his actions.

"Do you honestly believe that Harper can be trusted?" He stalks to his desk and opens a folder waiting for him on his desk.

"Did you trust me when we first met?" I ask, turning the tables on him.

He smirks, staring down at the pages, examining each one closely while speaking to me. "I knew who you were the first moment I laid eyes on you, kitten. Why do you think I chose the name Daniel?"

Approaching his desk, I smack his arm and roll my eyes. "You fucked me to get to my father." I always suspected that was the case, but I never heard him verbalize the truth. I want to be angry with him, but I honestly can't hate the man I'm married to.

He saved my life, protected me, and helped me raise our son.

Luca might not forgive Dante for all he's done, but

he is a decent father. Gino, my old man, was far worse to me.

"I'll admit, as much as you hate Harper, she did try to save that little boy, Rylan." There's quite a bit of tenacity in her, and Dante can't deny they are on the same side, even if Harper and Luca don't realize it.

"I don't hate her—" Dante says but lets the words linger in the air. "I just don't trust her. She could destroy everything, get us killed, or worse, betray us."

It's impossible to know how she'll react when she returns to campus. We can't keep her holed up in our home indefinitely. As tempting as it might be, her friends, family, they would all grow suspicious.

"Do you trust my judgment?"

"Implicitly," Dante says and glances up from the file, his fingers tangling in my hair as he brings my lips to his. "I've always trusted you; it's you who hasn't always trusted me," he reminds me.

"That was a long time ago," I say, "when we first met." I smile against his lips and pull away. "What you're doing with Rylan—it's noble but misguided."

"I didn't ask for your advice—" he says, glaring at me, but he's not angry. I've seen his angry glare, and it's nothing like what he's doing. His gaze is heated with lust more than anger.

"You brought him into our home, under our roof. You swore you'd never be involved in hurting children or trafficking them."

"I'm not!" He looks exasperated. "Do you think I have another option? I ordered a hit on his father, the man who *is* trafficking children, responsible for raping dozens of underage girls—children. I'm sorry if his son got mixed up in this, but his family and his home is going to be razed, and the only way to guarantee the child was safe was to bring him here."

I press my lips together, saddened that this was the only option. "That boy will grow up one day to be a man, and he's going to hate us," I say, warning Dante of the danger he puts our family in, whether he intends to or not.

He pulls back from me, his eyes burning. He barely slept last night.

He's not the only one robbed of sleep. After Moreno stormed into the room, awakening us and catching

Dante up to speed while he got dressed, I couldn't sleep.

I worried for my son, that Luca would get himself killed.

Dante doesn't always have a level head, and while Moreno tries to keep shit from blowing up in both of their faces, this time was far worse for all involved.

"What am I supposed to do? The hit is scheduled for tomorrow night. I can't just return the boy to his home. He'll be killed with them."

"And what's your plan after his family is dead?" I ask. Sometimes I wonder if Dante fully thinks through the logistics of his actions. I love him, but sometimes his stubbornness gets in the way of protecting his family.

"I was going to have him find his way to the police."

"Right, so he could identify you, our men, our home?" I'm not buying his story. "Dante, what the hell were you planning on doing with Rylan?"

"I was going to raise him as our own. Let them think he died in the explosion. The remains will be unidentifiable. They'll assume he perished. With time, he'll forget his past, his family, all of it."

"He's not an infant. He'll remember his family, and the prison, the fear that you've invoked in him. Do you really think he'll grow up as our son? What you're suggesting is absolute madness. He could have other family—grandparents, an aunt or uncle."

"I've already looked. There is no one else. He'll end up in foster care. You said it yourself, Nikki. We can't let him lead the police to our home. He's seen our faces, which leaves the only viable options—he belongs to us or we kill him."

"For fuck's sake, Dante! We're not killing a child."

"Then I guess it's settled. He shall be our son."

I throw my arms up in the air. "You can't just demand that and it becomes reality." I remember the trauma that Nova had, how she'd been mute, and it took time to trust again.

"Besides, he sees us as his kidnappers. What happens next? You suddenly let him free, save him?"

"No, you will," Dante says to me. "You'll raise him, let

him realize that we're not to be feared, and with time, he will forget what happened in the cellar."

"You're wrong. He won't forget. You can't just erase his memories."

"Tell me what you would do," Dante says, his fingers reaching out to push the hair back from my face. "If you were don, how would you handle this little situation?"

"I wouldn't have started with putting him in the prison basement!"

Dante winces, perhaps realizing his mistake. "He was only supposed to see Caden." One liability could have been easily erased. "Harper fucked everything up when she came down those stairs. What would you do *now*?" he asks.

"Blaming Harper was your first mistake. *You* should have kept out of that basement and let only Caden and whoever else recaptured him into the prison. You were too busy worrying about your son's involvement and the girl he likes, to think clearly," I say.

"Anyone else, and I'd kill them for talking to me that way," Dante scoffs.

"Well, you asked," I say, not the least bit afraid of my husband. I've lived with him long enough to know his good moods from bad. He's displeased but not ready to commit murder.

"I asked what you would do now, not what I did wrong," he says. He huffs and turns his back, returning his attention to the file on his desk, filled with pages on Harper McKenna. Everything from her social media accounts, posts, texts, emails, medical, and hospital records. It's more than just your typical background check.

I pause, considering all the options and variables. "I would take Rylan upstairs, sit him in front of the television and let him watch the news. Let him see when the explosion makes the news, and he realizes his family and everyone he knows is dead."

"Cruel," Dante whispers, tilting his head at me. "You do have mafia blood in you."

"I don't suggest it to be cruel, only for him to realize that he has nowhere to go, and that we saved him."

"He'll blame us," he says.

Dante is right. Rylan will blame us, but maybe we

deserve the blame. We're not innocent in all of this, and I don't pretend to be a saint.

"There's always Rhys," I say, pursing my lips as I consider the implication of what I'm about to suggest. "Rhys and Rylan haven't met. You ordered Rhys to remain outside of Nova's door last night, am I correct?"

"Rhys is always protecting Nova," Dante says. "He's practically her own personal bodyguard."

"Precisely. He's good with kids. He knows how to protect them, and we could stage an escape where Rhys rescues Rylan. Then he takes him to a shitty motel, and they can witness the destruction of his family on the news. At which point, he'll trust Rhys, and you can give them both new identities."

He strokes his jaw as he considers my suggestion. "That's not bad, except Rhys isn't going to be thrilled with the new assignment. Full-time father to a kid who isn't his?"

"Bump his salary and send them both to the Caymans or Costa Rica. Let Rhys have an early retirement when he's done with raising Rylan. Rhys will do whatever you ask of him," I say. "He's a good soldier."

"It's asking a lot," Dante says, realizing the weight of what he's done, "but I think it'll work."

His attention returns once again to the file, which is now spread out on his desk, pages upon pages.

I glance over his shoulder, reviewing the information in front of us.

Harper McKenna.

He ran a background check on the girl, not a huge shock.

"Anything interesting?" I ask, perching myself at the edge of the desk.

"Yes," he says and drags his finger over the highlighted portion that he wants me to read.

My breath catches in my throat as our eyes meet.

It seems Harper has been keeping a secret of her own.

SIXTEEN

HARPER

I don't want to have dinner with Luca's parents, but it seems I'm out of options.

"It'll be fine, just be yourself," Luca whispers as I bring my bag downstairs. After dinner, Luca is planning on driving us back to campus.

Ashton took the bus back to campus. He made it clear he didn't want to be part of tonight's dinner, but I think it was really Luca telling him to get his ass out of the house.

The tension between Ashton and Luca has been mounting since last night, and I don't think it's going away anytime soon.

I'll be relieved to return home, but it's not without scars and nightmares. And there's little I can do for the child tucked away in their basement. I need a plan, one that involves not getting caught, and that's impossible with the number of guards around the clock.

As for the engagement, I haven't reached out to my parents yet. I'll do that next week when I have to invite them to the Ricci's' for dinner.

I can't help but wonder if there's a way out of this mess, but I've yet to see it. Am I really going to marry Luca Ricci?

"Come on," Luca says, and he takes my hand, guiding me toward the dining room to have dinner with his parents.

I'm relieved to see Nova joining them at the table, but Moreno and Paige are also dining with us, and I'm hoping that maybe they can be the bigger distraction this evening.

"When you said family dinner..." my voice trails off.

"We're all family here," Moreno says, "better get used to it."

I exhale, and a sigh slips past as I make my way to one of the empty seats at the table where Luca pulls the chair back for me to sit. At least we're seated together. He gives my hand a squeeze before relinquishing it, reaching for his water glass.

"We'll cut past the formalities," Nikki says, her eyes entirely on me. "I'm well aware of the situation, that you're marrying my son to gain protection instead of death."

Her words cut deep, catching me by surprise.

"Mom!" Luca's eyes widen in disbelief.

"I'm just being honest, which I think is important, don't you, dear?" Nikki says as she stares at me.

I nod slowly. "Yes, honesty is important," I say, but I thought they didn't want me to be honest; they wanted me to hide the truth about what I saw in the basement. Isn't speaking honestly what was to get me killed?

"Good," Nikki says, and her eyes shine, but there's not quite a smile on her face. "I'm so glad we're on the same page." She laughs softly, glancing at Paige. "As your family, we expect complete transparency. Do you understand?"

"Mom?" Luca interrupts. "What are you doing?"

She holds up a finger, indicating that she's not done yet.

"Yes, I understand. Complete transparency with your family. Keep my mouth shut outside the family," I reiterate.

"Good. Now, is there anything you'd like to tell us or Luca?" Nikki asks.

I thought I liked Nikki, but the way she's staring at me, waiting for something—I'm not sure what—has me realizing that she's as cunning as her husband.

"I don't believe so," I say and glance at Luca. "Do you know what's going on?" I whisper to Luca.

He shakes his head no.

Did the child escape? Is that why the sudden line of questioning? Do they believe that I had something to do with it?

Dante frowns. "I'm disappointed in you, Harper. I had high hopes that this marriage arrangement would work, but if you're not being honest, you're going to find out quite quickly how we dole out punishments."

My hands tremble.

"I swear, I don't know what you're talking about."

Dante retrieves a file that has been sitting on his lap, hidden beneath the table. He opens the folder, the contents staring me straight in the face.

The air rushes out of my lungs.

No one was supposed to know.

"You failed to mention that you have a son."

To Be Continued.

The story continues in Between Ice and Oaths (Crimson Ice Book Two).

SHOP SPECIAL EDITIONS
& SIGNED BOOKS

THANK you so much for reading Between Blades and Blood. I hope you enjoyed the novel. Be sure to sign up for my newsletter for up-to-date new release details, sales, early release news, and more!

If you love signed paperbacks, special edition books, or discounted book bundles be sure to check out my online bookshop: https://shopwillowfox.com

ABOUT THE AUTHOR

Willow Fox has written in multiple genres. She's written everything from young adult dystopian to spicy RomCom novels. Her books have been translated into five languages and sold across the world.

Whether Willow is writing romance or sitting outside by the bonfire reading a good book, she loves the magic of the written word.

Follow her on any of her social media sites or through her newsletter!

Willow also writes kinky romance books under the pen name Allison West.

Visit her website at:

shopwillowfox.com

ALSO BY WILLOW FOX

Obsessive Boss

Dangerous Boss

Bossy Single Dad Series

Billionaire Grump

Mountain Grump

Bachelor Grump

Ice Dragons Hockey Romance

Faking it with the Billionaire

Daring the Hockey Player

Arresting the Hockey Player

Crimson Ice

Between Blades and Blood

Between Ice and Oaths

Between Fire and Frost

Between Sin and Silence

Between Steel and Secrets

Want more kinky romance? I also write under the pen name Allison West.

Gem Apocalypse Series

Emerald Rebellion

Amber Voyeur

Sapphire Sacrifice

Scarlet Assassin

Crimson Crown

Royally Claimed Series

Palace Secrets

Maiden Claimed

Grave Misfortune

Academy of Littles

Little Etta

Little Gigi

Little Eliza

Reforming the Rebellious

Little Lizzie's Reform (Little Lizzie)

Little Prim and Proper (Little Kat)

Virtue and Vice

A Proper Punishment (Little Lena)

Little Brides (Little Clara)

Dowries and Deception

Delia's Debt (Little Delia)

Decoy Bride (Little Vera)

Jessie's Secret

Violet's Penance

Piper's Escape

Fiery Luna

Little Jade

Little Alice

Little Love Bundle/Western Daddies

Little Samantha

Little Lexa

Little Autumn

Little Rosie

Prefer a sweeter romance with action and adventure?
Check out these titles under the name Ruth Silver.

Aberrant Series

Love Forbidden

Secrets Forbidden

Magic Forbidden

Escape Forbidden

Refuge Forbidden

Nightblood

Royal Reaper

Stolen Art